The Kantaberry Tales

By Derek Hawkins

authorHOUSE™

1663 LIBERTY DRIVE, SUITE 200
BLOOMINGTON, INDIANA 47403
(800) 839-8640
WWW.AUTHORHOUSE.COM

This book is a work of fiction. People, places, events, and situations are the product of the author's imagination. Any resemblance to actual persons, living or dead, or historical events, is purely coincidental.

© 2005 Derek Hawkins. All Rights Reserved.

No part of this book may be reproduced, stored in a retrieval system, or transmitted by any means without the written permission of the author.

First published by AuthorHouse 06/16/05

ISBN: 1-4208-3338-3 (sc)

*Printed in the United States of America
Bloomington, Indiana*

This book is printed on acid-free paper.

CONTENTS

GOTCHA 1
MAIL ORDER BRIDE 17
HUTIA 39
ROYAL ISLAND 55
VOODOO 77
TWO TEENS 91
BUGGIES 113
LAUNDRY 131
THE CURE 155
SHIP WRECK 177
THE DROP 207
SAFE SEX 221

Kantaberry (Phyllanthus Onorus) is a green leafed flowering shrub that grows exclusively on the islands of North Eleuthera. Similar to gorse that grows on the moors of Scotland, it too has yellow flowers that are replaced in the spring by dark blue berries the size of small grapes. The berries have been collected by the local people for centuries and their healing powers have become legendary. The below average incidence of heart disease, colon cancer, asthma and other common ailments among the residents of the communities of Spanish Wells, Harbour Island, Bluff, Upper and Lower Bogue has been attributed in part to their consumption of Kantaberry juice. It may also contribute to the peculiar traits evident in many of the residents.

GOTCHA

I had arrived in Spanish Wells on a forced vacation about a year and a half ago. I'd been told to get lost by my 'business' associates. I met a pretty girl, robbed the local bank, bought a yacht with the money, traded the yacht for some diamonds then sold the diamonds for a substantial profit, incriminated my best friend for the theft and returned the stolen portion of the money to the bank. A close buddy of mine wrote a best seller about the caper, named it 'Malice in Pinderland' and I thought that that was the end of it.

Boy was I wrong!

The sound of the judge's gavel still echoed in my ears as I heard him say, "Will the defendant please rise." It seemed as though I was in another world, an out-of-body experience. I slowly rose to my feet in unison with my attorney. I could hear my heart beating and I was sure that most of the assembled crowd in the courtroom could also hear it. I wasn't sure if I was supposed to look at the judge or hang my head in shame. It probably made no difference now anyway, his decision had been made; where I looked or how I looked didn't matter. All I could think of was let's get this over with; I'll face the music whatever it may be, but don't draw the decision out any longer. In actual fact I was quite calm. I suppose that when you are faced with the inevitable, when you are unable to have any effect on the result and know that there is absolutely nothing more you can do, there is no point in agonizing over the problem.

The Judge peered at me from his seat on the bench as if he was seeing me for the first time. Maybe he was, for during the brief trial, I had been convinced that for most of the time he had been asleep. I had hoped he had just closed his eyes to help with his concentration, but I knew I would always think about that and wonder if he had his mind made up long before my case came to trial.

"This has been a most unusual trial," he began. "The defendant may either be one of the most repentant men I've ever had the occasion to have in my court, or he may be one of the most foolish. I'm not sure. I hereby sentence you to three years!"

The Kantaberry Tales

One hundred and fifty six weeks! One thousand and ninety two days! If you say it quickly it doesn't sound like much, but if you're in the prime of your life, three years is a long time. Imagine waiting at the airport for a connecting flight that has been delayed for three or four hours; you know well the feeling of exasperation, the frustration over the waste of time. If you multiply this slight inconvenience to your schedule by a factor of five thousand, you'll have some idea of what I was feeling as the sentence was handed down. I'd be an old man by the time I was released. And what would my daughter think of me? And Melanie? Would she forgive me? Was it asking too much to expect her to wait?

"If you behave yourself and keep out of trouble, you could be out in eighteen months," my lawyer stated as I was led out of the courtroom. Annie, my daughter, and Melanie, my fiancée, were hugging each other as I glanced over my shoulder; they both gave me the thumbs up sign, which I took to mean that they would be waiting and that they thought three years wasn't so bad. Maybe they had been expecting me to be sentenced to ten years.

Fourteen months had passed since I had robbed the Royal Bank, and even though I had arranged for all the money to be returned, the Bank had insisted on pressing charges. I suppose I had broken into their property and I had shown them how vulnerable they were. My 'friend' Charlie Wolfsen, whom I had incriminated for messing around with my wife, had been ordered to leave the country and his estate on Harbour Island was now for sale. Melanie and I had purchased a nice beach front home in Spanish Wells, and she was hard at work establishing herself as an attorney from her office above the bank. We had actually picked a date for our marriage but had had to postpone the event when I was arrested.

My arrest came as a surprise to just about every one of the inhabitants of Spanish Wells, including me. I had settled into a daily routine on the island and had made many friends. Most of them thought that I was a bit of a hero for giving back the money and turning over a new leaf. At least that was the impression that I had. Melanie and I had decorated her new office and for a while I had acted as her receptionist until she had hired a local girl for the position. Her days were busy, she was happy and her happiness made me happy too. We lived in domestic bliss. I kept house, cooked the meals and generally waited on her hand and foot. By the time she came home I had dinner on the table. I'd learned how to cook soused chicken, stuffed shellfish, lobster thermidor and several other island specialties. The meat and potatoes diet that I had been raised on had been replaced with fish, grits, rice and 'Mac' and cheese.

The Kantaberry Tales

The fateful day was a Thursday. Two men arrived at my door and asked if they could talk to me. I had hesitated for a moment until one of them had routinely flashed his official badge in my face.

"What's this all about?" I asked innocently.

"We're from Canada," one of them responded, "Special Investigations Division of the RCMP."

They followed me into the living room, and at my invitation sat across from me at the dining table.

"We have a warrant for your arrest!"

"My arrest?" I stammered "but...."

"You thought we'd forgotten about you, eh?"

"Figured you'd gotten away with it, eh?" added the second officer.

"It's been more than a year," I stated in my defense.

"The authorities have been trying to decide which jurisdiction should prevail in your apprehension. The Bahamian police have the right to detain you, but as the bank you robbed is Canadian, it became clear that the Canadian authorities should be the ones to proceed with your arrest."

"But I'm British," I exclaimed in a frightened voice. I never thought that I would ever use that expression. I must have sounded like a character in an old British movie, yelling at the natives as they dragged him off to the boiling cauldron.

The two officers looked at each other with questioning expressions on their respective faces, as they digested this new piece of information.

"Then you'll probably be extradited to England for trial."

"How much time do I have?" I asked timidly.

The two officers had a whispered conversation together before the tallest one answered my question.

"Seeing as how there's no place to run to on this island, we'll trust you to meet us at the Ferry dock this afternoon at three. We'll travel to Nassau today and then we'll leave for Toronto tomorrow."

"And then?"

"We'll transfer you to the British officials and you'll be taken back to England, I suppose."

"On what charges?" I asked.

The shorter officer consulted the warrant he was in the process of handing to me, "Bank robbery!" he said.

The Kantaberry Tales

So that was that. I'd been nabbed!

I had less than five hours of freedom left. I felt crushed and for the first time in my life, I felt bitter. Sure, I'd been to prison before; it wasn't the fear of prison that bothered me, it was having to say goodbye to Melanie and my newly found peacefulness in Spanish Wells. At other times in my life a stint in prison was almost a welcome change from the hectic and highly stressful existence that came with my profession. But I had changed. I had left that life behind me. Now I had something to lose, somebody else to care about, somebody that I loved, somebody that I felt ashamed to have to admit to, that I had to leave to be incarcerated like an animal.

I called her office not knowing what I was going to say.

"Hello," the receptionist answered, "Melanie Pinder's law office."

"Hi Tara. It's David. Is Melanie there?"

"She's with a client. Do you want me to interrupt her?"

"No, ask her to call as soon as she's free. I'm at home."

I hung up the phone and wandered aimlessly around the house trying to make sense of the Bank's rationale. They had their money safe and sound. Nobody had been hurt and no damage had been caused. They must have pursued Charlie Wolfsen and he must have fingered me to save himself. It's what I would have done in his position. Maybe I'd meet him in prison. I actually laughed out loud at the prospect.

I slid open the glass doors at the back of the house and walked out into the garden. We had planted several exotic Kantaberry shrubs at the edge of the wooden deck and their colourful flowers and heavy scent reminded me of the fun that we had had shopping for them and then arguing about the best location to plant them. Their hallucinatory powers were legendary and I felt light headed as I walked the few short steps to the beach and watched as a few seagulls came circling overhead hoping that I had something tasty for them to eat. They would miss me too. I sat on old wooden bench that Melanie had painted bright pink, I placed my head in my hands and I cried.

I could hear the gentle lapping of the water as the tiny waves crept up the deserted beach with the incoming tide. I brushed away my tears and looked out towards Pierre Rocks where the sun was casting intricate shadows across their southern face. A lonely gull flew by, I watched with envy as it soared into the air on the breeze; it was as free as the proverbial bird. I would miss this wonderful place that I had come to call home.

I heard Melanie calling my name. I must have been meditating for longer than I had realized. I hurried back into the house.

"I called you several times but got no answer. Tara said you sounded sad, so I came home. What is it?"

Melanie looked beautiful in her business clothes. To me there was something sexy about the way she looked in a tailored suit, but then I thought that she looked sexy in just about any clothes that she wore. But that's just my biased opinion. I took her hand and led her to the sofa where I sat her down and kissed her. It was a kiss for the ages. Long and meaningful with all my desperate feelings released for a tender moment. I clung to her and sobbed like a baby.

"David. What's wrong?"

I didn't know how to tell her. I knew that she would be devastated. Our wedding day was approaching.

"Has something happened to Annie?"

"No," I cried, "it's not Annie. It's me. I've been arrested!"

Her immediate reaction was not what I would have expected from a bride-to-be. I could see that she was stunned and angry but she acted like the professional lawyer that she was.

"When and by whom?" she asked.

"About an hour ago by two RCMP officers. I'm to meet them at the dock this afternoon. They're taking me to Nassau, then to Toronto."

"Did they leave a copy of the warrant?"

"It's there on the desk," I indicated.

She found the warrant they had left and scrutinized it.

"It seems to be in order," she commented, "I'm coming with you. You'll need a lawyer."

"Melanie," I beseeched her, "listen to me, please. You're right, of course I'll need a lawyer, but this is not for you. I've already done enough to ruin your life without whisking you off to Canada and then to England on what we both know is a lost cause. I did rob the bank. I could never live with myself knowing that I had interrupted your new life here and your new law practice. I have a lawyer in England who'll be glad to represent me."

"The fact that you're guilty has nothing to do with your defense. In fact an admission of guilt and the repayment of the money should be enough to get you off Scot free."

"You don't really believe that," I said, "but that's not the point. I'm doing this my way and that does not include you as my counsel. Remember you could be considered as an accomplice and that risk is too much to even consider."

She weighed the impact of my words but she knew that I was right. Even though she was ready to accept the risk of being indicted as an accomplice, she knew that I would not allow it. I could see from the change in her facial expression that she had given in to my wishes and for the first time she had realized that our happy existence in Spanish Wells was about to come to an abrupt halt. Her eyes welled up with tears as this realization hit home.

"What about the wedding?" she mumbled through her tears "Will you come back?"

"If you'll have an ex con," I grinned.

"Just listen to me worrying about myself when it's you that'll be locked up. Oh David, how will you manage in prison with all those vile people?"

"It's not my first time," I answered, "I'm an old timer."

"But that was years ago. You were younger then."

I was trying to be brave, to put on an air of bravado, when in reality I was scared to death. Confinement in prison is a devastating experience at any age, but would be much more difficult to handle at my age. It had been almost twenty years since I had last been a guest of Her Majesty's Government and in those twenty years I had become a successful 'businessman' living a life of ease and comfort. In my previous incarceration I had treated the stay in prison as a vacation, as a brief interlude in my life when I could get my teeth checked, a free physical and three meals a day. Prison was a place where a petty crook like me learned how to become a hardened criminal. In those days I had not been lonely but now with my involvement with Melanie I knew that the nights would be long and unbearable.

"I could make a run for it," I said half jokingly. "Take the dinghy to Jeans Bay, a taxi to the airport or to Gregory Town, and then disappear!"

"Then I would come with you," she stated emphatically.

"It's tempting," I grinned, "I have enough money stashed in Switzerland for us to live on for the rest of our lives."

"Then let's do it."

"Melanie," I cautioned, "Be serious. We can't live our lives on the run."

"But I don't want to be parted from you for five or ten years or whatever the sentence may be. I'd rather live under a false identity and on the run with you than here on my own."

"It's not as though I'm a murderer or an international spy. I'm just a petty thief that gave the money back. I doubt that there would be much of an attempt to find me after a few weeks," I speculated.

"Sounds as though you're considering it."

"I wish we had more time."

"A few more hours would make no difference. If we're going, then let's go!"

I was on the verge of making a stupid decision when the phone rang. Melanie answered it and handed me the receiver. It was one of the Canadian officers calling to advise me that the Ferry would be leaving earlier than scheduled and that I should meet them on the dock in less than two hours. So that was that. There wasn't sufficient time to make a getaway. Our plan had been foiled.

"Who was that?"

"The police. I have to meet them earlier than planned. I have to go in an hour or so. There's no time to run."

Melanie burst into tears as the cold truth that I would be leaving finally registered. We had been together every day for more than fourteen months. We had become interdependent on one another and by choice we talked about everything that we did or watched or thought. We were tuned in to each others every whim or wish and I knew that the separation would be tough on her. Maybe tougher on her than on me, even though I was the one who was to be tried and probably locked away. I was older with a somewhat jaded perception of life and before meeting with Melanie I had been something of a loner. It was this attribute that I hoped would prepare me for the sentence and confinement that I was to face.

"You do know that I will come back," I said, "and you know that you don't have to worry about money. When I'm sentenced and settled I'll expect you to visit me. The time will pass quicker than you may think."

"I'll come for the trial," she sniffled.

"OK," I answered enthusiastically, even though I would have preferred her not to be there; it was my pride, I suppose, not wanting Melanie or anyone to see me in custody.

"I'm going to pack a bag," I mumbled.

"I'll help," she volunteered, as she followed me into our bedroom.

My thoughts were elsewhere so I was unaware that she was behind me undressing while I rummaged through my dresser drawers looking for clean underwear and shirts. I felt her arms around me as she clung to my back and pressed herself against me. Her hands wandered down between my legs where she hesitated for a moment to check to see if I was responsive.

"I'll miss my best friend," she whispered in my ear.

"And he'll miss you," I laughed.

She slowly undressed me.

Making love to her had always been exciting, but this time it was so different. We poured our emotions into each other with such passion that we both found it difficult to breath. As difficult as it was to find the words to express our feelings for each other at this time, it was far easier to say it with our actions. I could taste the salt of our tears on my tongue as I kissed her from the top of her head to the soles of her feet and all the places in between. I didn't want to stop and I didn't want to leave. I wasn't sure how I would survive without her, or whether she would continue to wait for me if I was gone for a long time.

It was time.

That old expression that there are no secrets in a small town applies in spades to Spanish Wells. How do the people on this island find out about things almost as fast as the participants themselves? There was a small crowd waiting at the dock. Some were seeing friends off as they too journeyed to Nassau, but most were there to take a last look at me. There was a mixture of well wishers, who genuinely felt sorry for Melanie and maybe for me, but most were there to observe, and I'm sure that some of the crowd thought that I was getting what I deserved. At least I would be the main topic of their conversations for a day or two.

The two policemen treated me with politeness and I would be forever thankful to them for refraining to put me in handcuffs. One of them gripped my arm as I was led up the ramp to board the Ferry.

As the Ferry left the dock and gathered speed it, passed by Abner's Golf Cart Rental, Pinder's Supermarket and the R&B Boatyard. I stood and waved a final goodbye to Melanie. I heard a few voices call 'Good luck' and a small cheer of support echoed through the air. I had never felt so forlorn and alone.

I wondered if I would ever see this idyllic place again.

MAIL ORDER BRIDE

Desmond Newbold checked his mailbox at three in the afternoon hoping that today would be the day that he would find a letter from his heart's desire. But it was empty. It had been empty for more than a month. But Desmond continued to check everyday, for he had faith and he knew that one day soon his dream would be realized and the girl of his dreams would be writing to him.

He wasn't a bad looking man. His best feature was his teeth. They were even and sparkling white just like those that he saw in the TV commercials for toothpaste. He had often thought that they were genetically handed down from his father because both his sisters also had picture perfect teeth... but not his mother. Hers were small and gray rather than white, a condition that made her speak with her mouth almost shut so that she avoided the embarrassment of showing her less than perfect molars. His father would often accuse her of being a contributor to his deafness. He had been asking her to repeat what ever it was that she had said all of their married lives because she mumbled through her closed lips, and now as he grew older he had grown into the habit of asking everyone that he met to repeat their conversations. His friends and family had wrongly assumed that he was going deaf when in actual fact it was just a bad habit that he had adopted.

Desmond would agree that he was a few pounds overweight but he knew that when Miss Right came along he would shed his love handles in a heart beat. He had a full head of hair that he kept stuffed under his Yankees baseball cap and a radiant smile that would melt the heart of the most somber funeral director in the Bahamas. He fished for a living just as his father and his uncles had been doing for a generation. He owned a share in the 'Blue Horizon', a white Ford pickup truck, a Yamaha wave runner, two building lots on Russell Island and three pairs of Nike sneakers. As he looked at himself in the mirror of his bathroom he grinned at his reflection and thought that he was a pretty good catch for any woman.

It had been a wet Saturday afternoon in July when Desmond had discovered his sister's computer. The summer months were his 'time off' when the fishing season was closed, and on this particular Saturday he had reluctantly agreed to baby-sit for his sister. The only sports that were being shown on television were golf and tennis and neither of these had any appeal for Desmond. His niece was sound asleep in her crib; he had checked several times just to make sure while he wandered aimlessly around the house looking for some relief from his boredom. The new computer was there in the bedroom, its screen alive with a whirling colorful screen-saver. He sat and watched the patterns, lines and colors for fifteen minutes before his eyes started to hurt.

Desmond would readily admit to the fact that he was not a computer whiz or even a person who had any interest in computers or their use. He would never admit that he was a little afraid of them and humiliated by many of his friends who had them and raved about their usefulness. He'd watched his friends play games, check their bank accounts and send messages to one another. The 'Blue Horizon' had a computer on board, so he was not totally unfamiliar with its use.

He casually pushed the mouse across the mouse pad which caused the screen-saver program to disappear and to be replaced by a Yahoo search engine. He sat down at the computer desk and clicked on the sports scores, then the weather report, then the news headlines, then the e-Bay auction. He found a site that sold Ford trucks, another that featured digital cameras, and then...Girls!

Girls from Russia! Girls from China! Girls from Cuba! Girls from every country on earth and all looking for husbands. Desmond felt as though he had hit the jackpot at the casino. He scrolled down the rows and rows of pictures and clicked on those that looked sexy, pretty, young and provocative. Two more clicks and their pictures were expanded to fill the computer screen. He saw his choices in bikinis, dresses, blue jeans and in some case almost no clothes at all. His mouth had gone dry as the pictures registered in his brain. His fingers were alive as they flashed across the keyboard to reveal more and more girls. His palms were sweating and his head was reeling as he thought of the possibilities of this newly found discovery.

He was so engrossed in his search that he never heard his sister arrive home. He almost jumped out of his skin when she said over his shoulder,

"That one's pretty."

"Jeannie. I never heard you come in. You scared me to death."

"What are you doin'?"

"Er, just foolin' around on the computer."

"Find anythin' interesting?" Jeannie laughed as her blue eyes quickly scanned the rows of girl's pictures that Desmond had selected.

"Don't you tell on me."

"I won't. You're not doin' anythin' wrong. You need a girlfriend."

"They're all looking for husbands. There must be thousands of 'em. Some of them are beautiful. Look."

Desmond clicked on his selections to reveal them in full size on the screen.

"This one's from Russia, twenty three years old, speaks fluent English, wants a family and wants to live where it's warm. She's really pretty. This one's from Latvia, wherever that is, she's twenty six, she's a teacher, went to college and loves the water. See, here she is on the beach. A knockout!"

"Go for it," commented Jeannie confidently, "nothing ventured nothing gained."

"You must promise that you'll keep it a secret."

"Course I will. Now what do you have to do next?"

"I dunno."

Desmond stood up and allowed his sister to sit at the computer. She quickly found the registration page and the rules and procedures. She printed them out and also printed out the bios on the girls that her brother had selected.

"You'll need some pictures of yourself to send with your letters or you can post a profile on their site and hope that one of them responds. You have to buy these girl's addresses. Six for seventy five dollars. That's only twelve fifty for a wife!"

"I'll buy 'em. But I don't need six."

"That's the deal. You gotta buy six. You've already picked out two winners; I'm sure that you can find four more. Good luck."

They heard a cry from the baby's bedroom and Jeannie left to take care of her daughter.

It took Desmond two hours to find the additional four prospects. He scrutinized every detail of each girl's features and became more and more selective as his criteria were honed to a fine edge. He carefully completed the registration forms and supplied his credit card information and Jeannie's e-mail address.

First thing Monday morning, Desmond presented himself at the local photography store for his pictures to be taken. He had given extra care to his appearance, having selected a clean T-shirt to go with his jeans, his favorite one with the picture of the dolphin in full color. He had decided to forgo his Yankees cap for such an important occasion, he'd borrowed his sister's magical kantaberry shampoo and his newly shampooed hair glistened on his head. In response to the inquiries from the photographer concerning the type and purpose of the pictures that he wanted, he had told a white lie and explained that he needed six pictures for several applications he was making for a new type of fishing license that he hoped to be awarded. He had felt very self conscious posing for the pictures and even though he knew that he should look happy and relaxed to impress his 'girls', he found it difficult to smile at the photographer. Since he had seen the girls in several different poses he decided that he too should have several pictures taken in different positions and with a variety of facial expressions. Pensive was a word that his sister had used, or carefree. He wasn't sure how to conjure his face to conform to his idea of what these expressions required. The result was that he looked rather like a fool in most of the pictures, but in two of them his own personality seemed to shine through and it was these that he and his sister selected to send off with his letter of introduction.

He had spent hours composing his letter. It was the first letter that he had ever written. He knew what he wanted to say. But he couldn't find the words. He wanted the 'girls' to understand that he was not a lecherous person, that his motivation was not driven by sexual desires, that he was a genuinely nice person with dreams and aspirations of finding the perfect companion and settling down to raise a family. He thought that it was important for him to describe Spanish Wells, to let them know that there were no theaters or sophisticated restaurants, no night clubs or bars and that the people were friendly and one big happy family. But he couldn't find the words. He needed to tell them how he worked hard, how she would have to understand that he would be away from home for long periods of time and how she would have everything that any woman could want and that he would love her and protect her and take care of her. But he couldn't find the words.

This is what he wrote:-

My name is Desmond Newbold, I live in a place called Spanish Wells. It's an island in the Bahamas. You sound nice and I would like to marry you, if we hit it off. PS, I'm 33.

Later on Monday his sister called to tell him that an e-mail had arrived from the agency. He rushed over to his sister's house and downloaded the e-mail to her printer. There were six profiles of the girls that he had selected, each one had an address, four had strange telephone numbers and two had e-mail addresses. He discarded the idea of sending an e-mail because it seemed too impersonal, plus he would never be able to compose an e-mail letter in addition to his letter of introduction. Telephoning was just out of the question; what could he be expected to say?

His next major problem was how to send the completed letters, each of which contained one of his pictures, through the mail. In Spanish Wells there is just one Post Office and Desmond went to school with the postal clerk and he knew that she would be very suspicious when he arrived with six letters to be sent to Russia. How could he discover how many stamps that each letter would need without raising any suspicions? He found his answer in the telephone directory where postal rates for every country in the world were listed. Russia was eighty cents for half an ounce. He bought the six eighty cent stamps that he required and carefully attached one to each of his precious envelopes. He knew that if he mailed them from the local post office there was a strong possibility that one of the postal workers would notice six letters with eighty cent stamps on them and their curiosity would lead to an unearthing of his secret. He couldn't take that chance. He carried the letters home with him to think of a safer way of sending them. It was his sister Jeannie who provided the solution. She was traveling to Briland the next day and she offered to carry the letters for her brother because, as she had said, she had an inclination of his dilemma. He could now rest easy in the knowledge that only his sister knew of his secret.

He pinned the six photos of his chosen partners to his bedroom wall adjacent to his bed where he could study their faces each night before he went to sleep.

The six girls were named, Katrina, Mariana, Anna, Oksana, Betina and Elena. He would often lay awake fantasizing about each of them and he even practiced and rehearsed the conversations that he might have with them. He decided that Oksana was his favorite but he would settle for any one of them.

He calculated that it would take ten days for his letters to reach their destinations so he circled the day on his calendar when he estimated that the girls would be reading his letters and studying his picture. He also calculated that if they chose to reply, they might do so in less than a week after receiving his letter, which meant he might receive a response during the next two weeks. He circled this day on his calendar in red.

His 'red letter' day had come and gone and still there was no letter, but just like clockwork he checked his mailbox every day.

Jeannie figured that the whole concept was an internet fraud and that he should report the agency to the proper authorities, but Desmond was too embarrassed to consider such a step. He was quite prepared to kiss his seventy-five dollars goodbye rather than let the whole community know of his innocent naivety.

Two more weeks passed. It was while he was drinking a soda outside the Gap that his friend from the post office called from her car as she passed by.

"Desmond, you've got mail. Letters from Russia!"

A chorus of wonderment came from his soda guzzling friends as they all were surprised to learn that he had mail of any kind, let alone mail from Russia.

Three letters had arrived at the same time. He studied the stamps and the hand writing as he carried them gingerly back to the privacy of his bedroom where he could read them at his leisure and away from the eyes of his curious friends.

He opened the one from Oksana first. His heart was in his mouth as several pictures fell from the envelope. Her letter was two pages long, written in a stylish form on pale blue paper. There was a scent of perfume on the pages.

Dear Desmond,
I thank you for your kind letter and the picture that you enclosed. I think you look like a very honest man and happy.

Derek Hawkins

I'm glad to see that you are happy, because I too am a happy person by nature and would not be interested in a serious-minded person. I looked for the Bahamas on a map but could not find Spanish Wells, is it a little island? I would love to live in a warm country because as you can imagine it is very cold here for most of the year. I thought that you looked younger than thirty three because you have such a lot of hair, with no gray. Do you dye it?

Would you please send me more information about yourself? What you read? What kind of music you like? Your favorite food? Do you have any brothers or sisters? Do you live in a house or an apartment? Do you have a girlfriend there?

I too would like to find the right man to marry. In Russia all the men are like pigs; they treat us badly. I am enclosing some more pictures, these were taken very recently, and my e-mail address. It will be easier to send letters via email than by snail mail. I envy you being surrounded by nice warm water. Do you have beaches there? I hope you will find time to reply and that you're not married to someone else. I'm waiting for your letter.

The letter was signed Oksana.

Desmond read the other two letters. One was from Betina that simply thanked him for his letter but said that she was writing to inform him that she was now engaged to be married.

The Kantaberry Tales

The third letter was from Katrina. It was a nice friendly letter but the picture that she had enclosed showed her playing with her two children, something that Desmond had not bargained for. He was sure that she had omitted this information in her profile.

He read Oksana's letter again and again. Her new pictures were of better quality than those that he had retrieved from the internet and showed her to be even more beautiful than he could have imagined. At that very moment he knew that he was in love for the first time in his life and that this pretty girl from Russia would become his wife.

He had to tell someone his news. Jeannie was off the island so he couldn't tell her. He gathered up the letter and the new photographs and rushed down to the Gap, where several of his friends were congregated.

"I'm gettin' married," he proclaimed to them all, as he burst through the front door.

They all looked at him as if he had lost his senses. Then the barracking and the questions began.

"To who?"

"Who'd have you?"

"You must be joking!"

"What are you smoking? Kantaberry weed?"

"I am, I am. See, here's her picture."

The pictures of Oksana were passed around from hand to hand.

"She's really somethin'."

"A Russian, eh? Does she have a sister?"

"Boy, she's pretty".

Desmond opened her letter and read from the pages informing all those present that she had said that she wanted to get married, that she wanted to live in a warm country and that she thought that he looked younger than his age.

"But you haven't actually met her?" someone asked.

"Not yet, but I'll invite her to come for a visit,"

"She'll expect you to pay."

"Of course."

"What happens if you don't like her, or if she doesn't like you?"

"It won't be like that. We'll know all there is to know about one another before she comes."

"Make sure that you tell her the truth about yourself and about Spanish Wells. If you paint too rosy a picture she'll be disappointed and she'll want to go home. And you better hope that she's telling you the truth."

Several of Desmond's friends came to shake his hand or to give him a friendly slap on the back.

"We're happy for you" they shouted in unison as he left.

Desmond learned how to send e-mails on his sister's computer. He had to use her e-mail address and her password, but he felt comfortable in the knowledge that he could trust his sister implicitly. Oksana sent at least one letter every day and over the next few weeks he came to understand everything about her. Her dreams and aspirations, her idiosyncrasies, her history, her family and slowly the sweetness of her nature was revealed. Desmond became more explicit with his correspondence and he began to find the right words as he described himself and Spanish Wells to Oksana. It was exactly six weeks to the day after he had received that first letter from Oksana, that he added a short sentence to one of his e-mails...Will you marry me?

Her reply came back immediately....Oh yes!

Desmond was apprehensive about flying to Russia. For one thing he had never flown anywhere, and secondly he had heard too many unsavory stories and seen too many movies about people crossing into Russia. Oksana's country of birth was a very long way from the Bahamas and would entail three or four changes of airlines and take two or three days to complete; a daunting challenge for any first time flyer. She offered a solution.

I have a sister who lives in London, she wrote. I could fly to England and stay with her for a while and you could come to London to meet me. We can spend some time together there, before flying to the Bahamas.

He agreed immediately, thinking that once again he was living a charmed life as everything had continually fallen into place as if his destiny was being guided from above. British Airways flew from Nassau to London every Friday and it would be a simple and easy flight.

They picked a date that was convenient for them both. Desmond offered to send the money for her flight from Russia to London but she assured him that she could manage. She did write to say that she thought that he was very considerate and kind in making the offer and that these were two qualities that she really admired in a man.

The arrangements were completed. Oksana would fly into London on Wednesday to stay with her sister and Desmond would leave Nassau on Friday and arrive in London on Saturday morning. Oksana said that she would phone from England on Wednesday when she arrived. Desmond walked around with his feet barely touching the ground. He just couldn't believe his luck.

He kept one of her pictures in his wallet and whenever he was alone for a few moments he took it out of the wallet and gazed at her pretty face. Everyone in town knew about his upcoming trip and his obsession with the Russian girl. The majority of the townsfolk were happy for him and pleased that he was finally getting married, but a few people thought that he should have found a local girl rather than to go searching for a wife halfway round the world. And a communist to boot!

The days passed quickly as Desmond sought to buy cloths for his trip and his meeting with Oksana. Jeannie convinced him that he should wear something other than T-shirts with pictures of fish on them and went with him to Three Sisters to buy a selection of collared shirts, new underwear, polyester pants and a jacket. He refused to buy a tie and he never understood why his sister insisted on making him buy uncomfortable leather shoes with hard soles when he already possessed three pairs of Nikes. The Nikes cost a lot more than the leather shoes he rationalized, so what could be wrong with them? He stayed home all day on Wednesday to wait for the phone call. With the five hours difference in the time between England and the Bahamas, he expected the call could come at any time in the day. It came at two o'clock.

The phone only rang once.

"Hello," Desmond said nervously.

"Hi," a voice replied "it's me."

There was a short pause as they both waited for the other one to speak; when they did they both spoke together which caused some nervous laughter that broke the ice.

"You first," suggested Desmond.

"I'm here, in London and its raining. I'm at my sister's home. She's got two kids that I haven't seen for a couple of years. They're so big now. Are you excited?"

"I thought that you would have an accent, you know, like a Russian spy in the movies. You speak perfect English!"

After a moments hesitation she continued "I attended an English immersion school and I've spent quite a lot of time in London with my sister. I could speak with an accent if you would like me to."

"No, its fine, but it wasn't what I was expecting. My friends are giving me a big party tomorrow night, a send off."

"I'll give you my sister's address if you have a pen. It would be best if you came here directly from the airport."

Desmond found a pen and a scratch pad and carefully wrote down the address as Oksana dictated it. It would be his only connection to her when he arrived. He read it back to her for her confirmation.

"How is the weather there?" she asked.

"It's only nine in the morning but the sun is out. It's about eighty degrees."

"I can't wait to be there. I'd better go 'cause this is my sister's phone. I'll see you on Saturday....I love you."

"Me too....Bye."

And she was gone.

"Who was that on the phone?" called Jeannie from the kitchen.

"Oksana," replied Desmond, "she called to let me know that she's in London at her sister's."

"What did she sound like?"

"She spoke perfect English. No trace of an accent."

"Oh really," commented Jeannie in disbelief.

"Yes. She also said that she loved me."

"So she should. You're a fine catch."

The 'send off' party at the Gap turned out to be a much larger event than Desmond's closest friends had expected. More than a hundred people showed up to wish him well and to express their support of his initiative in finding a foreign bride. A poster size picture of Oksana had been fastened to the wall above the chair where Desmond sat and everyone agreed that she was as pretty as a picture. Desmond had never felt so proud. He finally left the party at midnight, vowing that he could not drink any more soda or eat any more fritters. He thanked everybody for coming and for their good wishes and said with a big grin on his flushed face that he would be back in a week with his future wife.

On Friday he caught the Ferry to Nassau for the first stage of his journey to England. He had packed all his new clothes in a suitcase that he had borrowed from Jeannie. He had a gift for Oksana wrapped in glossy silver paper with a big silver bow on it. The gift was from Jeannie. 'It's something sexy' is all she would tell him. The only other gift he carried was a ring. Even Jeannie didn't know about it. He had paid one of his friends to buy it for him at the John Bull store in Nassau and now it was tucked safely in the pocket of his new polyester pants.

There was a small crowd to see him off at the dock. He kissed Jeannie and thanked her for her help and her silence. He waved as he walked up the boarding ramp and took a last look at Spanish Wells.

Jeannie drove home from the dock, made sure that her daughter was sound asleep, picked up the telephone and called England.

"He's on his way," she said.

There was a short pause as she listened to the voice of Oksana's 'sister'. Then she said. "I thought I'd never get rid of him. He's finally out of the house. I can hardly believe it. But your 'sister' almost blew it, talking without an accent; even my dumb brother was suspicious. I hope that she's a nice girl and that she does look something like the pictures you sent."

HUTIA

Just a short boat ride from Spanish Wells is the northernmost coast of Eleuthera. It was here in 1648 William Sayles and his Eleutheran Adventurers, a group of English Puritans, arrived seeking a land where they could find freedom to work and to worship their God as they saw fit. One hundred and fifty seven of them came ashore after their ship was wrecked on the Devil's Backbone, a treacherous series of reefs that protect this northern shore from the brunt of storms and hurricanes that periodically ravage this coast. Sayles and his friends lived in caves which are still in evidence in this area, for almost two years before migrating to Spanish Wells and Harbour Island. They held religious services in the Preacher's Cave, a large cave with a high ceiling that still remains intact. Work is scheduled to begin soon by the Bahamas Historical Society to excavate the floor of the cave and the surrounding land.

Today most of the land in this area is uninhabited. While mostly scrub, there are several local farms where citrus fruits are grown. Many of these farms are owned by the people of Spanish Wells and are farmed by their Haitian employees.

The beach that stretches for miles along this northern shore is desolate, untouched and pristine. It was the favorite get-away location for Michelle and her friend Jacques.

Their parents had escaped from the poverty of Port-au-Prince on a small over-crowded boat, seeking similar goals to those Eleutheran Adventurers who had escaped to the Bahamas, almost four hundred years before them. After being shipwrecked in the Southern Bahamas they had been transported to Nassau where they were processed through immigration, issued legal papers and sent to Eleuthera as farm workers. Michelle and Jacques had both been born a year later and had spent all their lives in this unique and spectacular area. Each day they caught the ferry from Jean's Bay to Spanish Wells where they attended The Spanish Wells All Age School.

They were excellent students, both eager to learn and to take advantage of this opportunity that their parents never had.

They wore their school uniforms with pride and were always careful to be polite to all the people that they met in Spanish Wells.

On Sundays they attended Catholic Church in a dilapidated building that served their small Haitian community as a place of worship. Michelle and Jacques were happy kids. They enjoyed the isolation that North Eleuthera provided and they relished living in the primitive desolation that they shared with God's creatures.

From Bridge Point at the western end of the coast of North Eleuthera to Hawk's Point to the east was a distance of about a mile, and if you counted them there were at least five wonderful beaches that included Platter Bay, Tay Bay and Gallow Bay. Michelle and Jacques had grown up on these beaches, learning how to body surf on the waves, finding the hidden nests of the turtles, swimming beyond the breaking waves to locate fish and lobsters among the coral heads and watching the sea birds mate and nest during the spring. They were attuned to the changes in the weather, the migrating patterns of the birds and fish and the eating habits of the many creatures that made these beaches, reefs and rocks their homes.

Few visitors ever came to their natural playground and those that did usually came by boat and spent their time on the beach. They never ventured inland. The Fast Ferry navigated the deep channel inside of the Devil's Backbone twice a day and came within twenty feet of the beach as it carried tourists and locals between Spanish Wells and Harbour Island. Michelle and Jacques often raced along the beach as the Ferry passed to the enjoyment of the passengers and crew. They were photographed hundreds of times and unbeknownst to them those pictures were prized and scrutinized by the families and friends of those tourists that had made the trip.

Jacques was a tall sensitive boy with an inner strength that set him apart from other boys of his age. He had earned the respect of all his neighbors, and his superior knowledge of all creatures both large and small had placed him in a position of adviser to both farmers and fishermen. It was rumored that his slender hands had the power to heal animals and that even rabid and ferocious dogs became passive when he touched them. He would never consciously kill any living creature and when he walked he was always careful to watch that he did not inadvertently step on an ant or a spider. Birds with broken wings and goats with broken legs were brought to him for repair and with the aid of his lifelong friend Michelle, he fashioned splints, slings and supports to help the stricken animals.

It was the day after a rage, a sea condition that was known locally by this term, when the Atlantic rollers crashed against the reef and turned the sea into a white frothy maelstrom, that they discovered a large Hawksbill turtle stranded on the beach. The turtle was near death. One of its flippers was dangling and another was bleeding from a wire fishing line that was wrapped tightly across its back and around its flippers. Unable to swim, the turtle had been washed ashore where it gasped for breath in the sand.

Jacques was quick to react to the disaster

"Michelle, run as fast as you can to the house and fetch a pair of pliers and my bag."

Michelle had already assessed the situation and took off like a bat out of hell to fetch the tools. While she was gone Jacques carefully stroked the turtle's head, making sure that he avoided its sharp beak, while he examined the damage. There was a deep cut that had almost severed the right front flipper and it was obvious that the turtle was losing a lot of blood. If he had to make a guess, Jacques figured it was about three years old and weighed fifty to sixty pounds. The steel wire had made a clean cut which would be easy to stitch and the salt water had ensured that the cut was clean.

Michelle came running at full speed along the beach with Jacques' bag slung over her shoulder. She was hardly breathing hard.

Jacques grabbed the bag, found the pliers and quickly cut the fishing line from around the flippers and from across the turtle's back. Michelle pulled the wire free as Jacques cut it.

"We'll have to turn him over," stated Jacques, "I can't stitch his flipper while it's in the sand."

They stood on either side of the wounded turtle and carefully placed their hands under the edge of its shell.

"Watch out for his beak," warned Jacques.

After several tries the two of them managed to turn the turtle onto its back. There was a triple-hook fishing lure fastened under its neck in an area close to its beak.

"Be careful," said Michelle as she watched Jacques reach for the lure. "One bite from that beak and you could lose a finger."

Jacques knelt in the sand close to the turtle and whispered quietly as he gently moved the pliers closer to the creature's mouth and neck. The turtles eyes lost their frightened look as Jacques voice seemed to mesmerize it. He cut the wire from the lure to release the strain and ease the pain, and then he gingerly twisted the hooks out of the turtle's neck.

While Jacques stitched the gaping wound in the flipper with nylon fishing line, Michelle carried water from the sea in an old jug and poured it over the turtle to keep him wet

"Now we have to wait. The bleeding has stopped but it will start again if he uses it to swim. Do you think that we can carry him to the pond?" Jacques asked.

"We have to," answered Michelle.

The pond was not really a pond but a pool that was left by a very high tide that always had a foot or two of water in it. They had used it to nurse crabs and lobsters back to health after they found them with broken legs or claws, but they had never used it for a big turtle. The pond was fifty feet from where the turtle was stranded.

They partially lifted and partially dragged the turtle across the beach, being careful not to touch the mended flipper. It was strenuous work for them but they made it.

They turned him over in the shallow water of the pool and watched as he cast his big eyes around his new home.

"We just have to hope that he's smart enough to stay put for a few days," commented Michelle.

"Oh he will," Jacques reassured her, as if he had communicated with the turtle in some way.

Three days later they sat and grinned at each other as they watched the turtle swim around the pool. The wounded flipper had healed and the turtle was ready to leave. He swam across the pool to where the two children were watching; he lifted his head out of the water and looked at them both with a look that could easily be interpreted as a look of gratitude. Then he heaved himself out of the pond, waddled down the beach to the water's edge and swam away.

"Goodbye," they called after him.

They watched until he disappeared into the deep water.

"Let's check the litter," suggested Michelle. "I want to take one to school tomorrow for show and tell."

The litter she referred to was a litter of three baby shrews they had found in a nest in a remote section of the land about a mile from the beach.

They walked home to find a box they could use as a temporary home for one of the babies. Without the aid of a compass or a GPS they walked through the dense bush where probably no one had ever walked before until they came to an old tree that had been hit by lightning many years ago. They walked under its broken branches and dropped to their knees to find the burrow where the little babies lived. Jacques was careful not to disturb the little nest as he transferred one of the little creatures to the ventilated box. He placed a selection of leaves, kantaberries and twigs that he knew was the diet of these shrews into the box as well. They had just stood up when Jacques caught Michelle's attention by placing his finger to his lips and indicating a spot to her left. There were the parents. They were wrestling with each other, grooming each other and tumbling around on the ground. They were the size of rabbits with beady eyes and long whiskers. After a few moments they scurried away.

"We must bring this little one back as soon as we can."

The next day Michelle carried the box with the baby shrew into class. When her turn came for show and tell, she proudly opened the box to show the teacher and the other students her treasure.

"It's a baby shrew," she told the class. "Jacques and I found a nest of them."

Miss Turner, the science teacher, looked into the box and asked, "Where did you find this?"

Michelle looked for support from Jacques. She was afraid that she had done something wrong.

Jacques answered for her. "On the mainland, between the beach and the road to the Cave."

"Did you see its parents," asked Miss Turner.

"Yes. We watched them tumbling around and grooming each other. They never saw us."

"And how big were they?"

"As big as a rabbit," replied Jacques.

"You're sure about this?"

"Yes Miss."

"And could you find them again?"

"Yes, we're goin' to put this one back as soon as we get home."

"I want you to go home now and put this baby back in its nest. If I'm correct, this is not a shrew. It's a Hutia!"

"A what?" the children all asked together.

"It's called a Hutia. It's practically extinct. There used to be lots and lots of them, but people shot them for their meat and dogs killed them and now there are none left. This is a wonderful discovery."

Later that day Miss Turner called Dr. Crestwell at the University of Miami to report her findings. His reaction was one of utter disbelief, but after she answered his detailed questions he was convinced enough to plan a trip to Spanish Wells to complete an investigation.

"You do realize that this creature was once exclusive to the Bahamas and was thought to be extinct until a few were discovered in 1966 in the Plana Cays in the Southern Bahamas."

"That's why I called you."

"And two Haitian kids found them?"

"That's correct."

"It's unbelievable. I can hardly wait to get there."

Three days later an entourage of scientists, journalists and cameramen assembled on the dock outside of the Customs Office in Spanish Wells. Miss Tucker introduced the two children to the group and in a loud excited voice asked Jacques to lead the way.

Michelle was overwhelmed by all the attention that she was receiving and huddled close to her friend in the hope that she could benefit from his calmness. Jacques surveyed the group and their equipment, placed his arm around Michelle's shoulder and with a calm and deliberate voice, explained their rules. Only Dr. Crestwell and Miss Tucker would be permitted to accompany them. All the rest would stay behind.

"You'll destroy the fragile environment with all of your equipment, your heavy boots and shoes, your cigarettes and food wrappings," he announced.

Their protests lasted for an hour but Jacques was firm. It would be two or none at all!

Jacques and Michelle had decided earlier that they would not take the most direct route to the little burrow, but instead would lead the Doctor and Miss Tucker on a journey along the beach before heading inland along a twisting trail that their compasses could never retrace.

By the time that the little procession reached the beach, the two visitors were panting and puffing from exhaustion.

As they crested a small rise that overlooked the long sandy beach, two small naked boys called to Jacques.

"Hi Jacques, we're nearly finished."

"Friends of yours?" asked Miss Tucker as she collapsed onto the sand for a rest.

"My little brothers," answered Jacques.

They watched as the two boys scrambled along the beach collecting the conch and starfish that the tide had washed ashore. They carried each one to the water's edge and carefully set them free. The long stretch of beach was littered from one end to the other with these stranded creatures.

"They can't possibly save them all," commented the Dr. "It's a waste of time."

They watched again as the smallest of the two boys carried two more starfish to the water and placed them where the tide would take them back to sea.

"Ask those two that Pierre just rescued if it was a waste of time," stated Jacques with contempt.

The Dr. and Miss Tucker looked at Jacques in amazement, while Michelle nodded in agreement.

Jacques told them to follow in his footsteps, suggesting that they place their feet in the spots where his feet had been planted. As they changed direction and moved away from the beach they were confronted by two families who had wounded animals with them. Jacques stopped to attend to the animal's problems before they continued on, not caring about the delay his ministrations caused. The visitors welcomed the rest.

"How much further?" asked the Dr.

"We're almost there," replied Jacques, "but from here the going gets rough, so stay close."

After a while Jacques held up his hand to halt the group. He signaled for Michelle to go ahead to the burrow while he made sure the others remained silent. Michelle checked to make sure that she was downwind from the spot and slowly with the utmost care she moved forward until she could peer over the low kantaberry bushes into the burrow. She signaled to Jacques that the Hutia were still there.

One by one they crept forward to observe the little babies. Both the Dr. and Miss Tucker carried cameras and they clicked off dozens of pictures. Jacques motioned for them to move away from the burrow and to hide behind the old broken branches of the tree that had been struck by lightning. When they were all concealed he started to hum, quietly at first, then a little louder. His eyes were shut tight as his voice echoed through the surrounding bush. Michelle was the first to see them. She tugged on Miss Tucker's sleeve and pointed to a clear space within the scrub where the male and female adult Hutia were grooming each other completely oblivious to the presence of the humans. The Dr. and Miss Tucker took a hundred pictures as the two Hutia wrestled with each other and played like two children.

They stayed for almost an hour watching in fascination as the two almost extinct animals frolicked in front of them. Jacques led the party away from the old tree and started on the return journey.

"Are we returning a different way?" asked the Dr..

"Yes," answered Jacques, "this way will take us past our home; we are supposed to be home by now. Our Mothers will be worried. I'll show you the road back to Jean's Bay where you can catch the ferry to Spanish Wells."

They walked in silence the rest of the way. They reached the shacks where the two families lived and before Jacques and Michelle could run inside, the Dr. stepped forward to shake Jacques hand.

"I'd like to meet your parents," he said "I have something to say to them."

"They don't speak much English."

"Then you can translate," the Dr. insisted.

None of their parents had ever entertained foreigners in their small homes and they were extremely apprehensive about meeting the teacher and the Dr., but Jacques persuaded them that it would be fine.

"You have two wonderful children," the Dr. stated, looking at the four parents who were assembled outside the shacks. "Your children are very gifted and I would like their help."

They waited as Jacques translated.

The Dr. continued.

"I would like to hire both Michelle and Jacques to continue with their surveillance of these animals and to report to me every week. I'll pay them each fifty dollars a week."

After Jacques translated this information to the four parents there was a lot of commotion and a lot of smiles.

"I would also like to offer each of you," the Dr. carried on, this time directing his conversation to the two children, "a full scholarship to my University when you become of age."

Jacques' Father, a short skinny man with very few teeth in his mouth, who up until this moment had not said a word for fear of embarrassment over his lack of knowledge of the English language, stood and grinned at the Dr.

There was a quiet pause of expectancy as the small group waited for him to say something profound. After a few thoughtful moments he extracted two words from his limited vocabulary of less than fifty words and said in a loud and triumphant voice, "Holy shit!"

ROYAL ISLAND

Johnnie Cormac had almost been born with a silver spoon in his mouth. I say almost, because both his uncles had, his Aunt Maisy had and at least five of his cousins had. There were probably many more relatives that he didn't even know the names of, who had also been blessed with unearned fortunes and a life of ease. But he had received nothing. His lineage was illegitimate, his heritage was tainted, and as his great grandmother had told him on her death bed, her side of the family had no claim to the family fortune. But why? He had never understood. All that he had received from her was a worthless fragment of an old hand drawn map that she herself had inherited from her great grandmother.

Derek Hawkins

This was a huge family with its roots in Ireland but its branches in every state in the East, from New York to Florida. Not all of them were Cormacs. The name had changed over the centuries and included McCormac, MacCormick, Cormack, Carmack and a host of similar surnames. The one thing that they all had in common was an ancestor that they could all trace back to South Carolina and the early eighteenth century. The source of their good fortune was from the estate of a smart Irish lawyer who ran away from his wife and the family home in Kinsale, County Cork, in the 1690's, with his wife's pretty personal maid, then settled in South Carolina. Here he assembled a large plantation, buying out his neighbors whenever the opportunity arose, planting cotton and later on tobacco, treating his workers like slaves and rewarding his foremen for record harvests regardless of the brutality that they afflicted to gain the result. He was prolific in the bedroom and on the plantation, siring many children and breeding many horses. Only one of his children had been born in Ireland and had accompanied him on the pilgrimage to South Carolina. This was his daughter Anne. She was fifteen when they settled in their new land. She missed the alleys, pubs and people of Dublin and she would often find her way to Charleston where she sought out 'her kind of people'. She was a strikingly beautiful girl with long black hair and fiery blue eyes, but she cursed like a sailor and fought like a banshee.

It was in Charleston that she met Jimmy Bonny, a drunken sailor who charmed her into marrying him with the idea of securing a better way of life for himself by convincing Anne to lay claim to that part of her father's plantation he felt was rightfully hers. Mister Bonny seriously underestimated her father, who promptly disowned his sixteen year old daughter and threw both of them out into the street.

For almost a year they remained in Charleston where they eked out a living by stealing from the businessmen on the streets or by robbing drunks during the night. Anne had learned how to use a knife and a sword and she could hold her own with the roughest of the seamen who habituated the taverns on the waterfront of Charleston. With her saucy good looks and her quick wit, she was a favorite of all the men and it was rumored that she had been known to grant certain favors to those captains and seamen she thought could be useful to her in the future. Her husband had become a third rate pirate on a vessel that was commanded by Charles Vane. In the fall of 1717 the boat left Charleston bound for Nassau. Anne was on board.

Yvonne Provost met Johnnie Cormac at Riverbend Marina in Fort Lauderdale. She worked as a finisher. A finisher is a person that sands and varnishes wooden trim on sailboats after the carpenters have completed their repairs or when the woodwork has begun to peel from too much exposure to the elements.

Johnnie had saved his money and had purchased an Irwin thirty-two foot sloop. It needed a lot of work, which he had decided to perform himself, even though he had very limited experience in fixing old boats. He spent all of his spare time and all of his money at the boatyard and was usually there until late into the evening. He had noticed Yvonne when he first arrived. She was easy to notice. She worked in the sun all day beneath a large straw hat and little else. It had taken him three weeks to pluck up the courage to ask her out for a drink. A drink was about all he could afford. She was from Quebec and spoke English with a cute French accent. She was working at the Marina illegally for cash, hoping to find a better job and a way to become a US resident. They had a couple of beers at the Southport Raw Bar and then they split an order of fries. He asked her out again the following Friday and this time they walked by the New River, admiring all the fancy yachts moored there.

"I'll have just as much fun on my little boat as any of these people," he stated emphatically.

They stopped to sit on a bench beneath a large flowering tree.

The Kantaberry Tales

"I'm heading for the Bahamas when I've finished her," he said.

"On your own?" she asked coyly.

"That's my plan. Why? Would you like to come along?"

"Yes. But I hardly know you."

"I won't be ready to leave for another month. We'll have time."

And they did. They saw a lot of each other and came to realize that they both had similar expectations from life. They both came from the wrong side of the tracks, from simple families, and their motto was to live each day as best they could and to be happy. Nothing could have been simpler. They saved a few dollars each week that they would use as an emergency fund and with just the clothes on their backs they launched their little sailboat that Yvonne had christened 'Soleil', and headed east to Gun Cay and the Bahamas.

They made landfall after a slow fourteen hour crossing, dropped their danforth anchor in Honeymoon Bay and celebrated with their one and only bottle of cheap white wine. Dom Perignon could not have tasted any better.

"This is the life," murmured Johnnie as he sipped his wine from a plastic cup.

The full moon cast a beam of light across the tranquil water of the bay that silhouetted the 'Soleil' as she quietly moved against the anchor. There was no wind and the temperature was still in the eighties.

"I will sleep on deck tonight," said Yvonne, "it's so pretty."

"You'll wake up soaking wet from the dew."

"So, it will be like a shower, eh?"

"Don't say I didn't warn you."

Johnnie left her on deck and went below to sleep. They were both tired from the long trip and the exhilaration of reaching the Bahamas without incident. The convertible bed in the main salon was barely big enough for two, so Johnnie had been pleased that Yvonne had chosen to sleep on deck. He dropped his shorts onto the floor and slid between the sheets. He was asleep in no time.

Yvonne could not find a comfortable position on deck. Even with the cockpit cushions as a mattress she still fidgeted as she tried to fit her slender body between the mast stays and the gunnel. Eventually she dozed off only to awaken after a while to find that she was wet and cool. Yvonne almost never wore any clothes, certainly not to sleep in, and only in the daytime when they had company or were in close proximity to other boats.

She finally gave in and crept below. She lifted the covers and slid into bed with Johnnie. She snuggled into his body to get warm and soon she too was fast asleep.

They had no plans. Many of the decisions on where to go and in which direction to sail were determined by the wind. They fished while underway and snorkeled around the coral heads for food when they anchored. They had both become efficient divers and they grew healthier on their diet of conch, crawfish and crab. For the first two weeks they never met a living soul; it was as if they were the only people on the planet. They had never been happier and their happiness cemented their relationship into a cohesive understanding of each other's needs. They knew when one of them needed to be alone or when one of them was homesick. They read the signals and acted accordingly. Although neither of them ever discussed the subject it was obvious that they had fallen in love. It was just three weeks after arriving in the Bahamas that they found the beautiful protected anchorage at Royal Island.

Jack Rackman was the quartermaster on board Captain Vane's pirate ship the 'Treasure'. Jimmy Bonny was one of the crew but it was his wife Anne who had secured him his position. Bonny was a useless drunk, unable to function as a crew member or as a husband. Rackman had his roving eye on

Anne, and by keeping her worthless husband around, thought he might be able to have his way with her. The 'Treasure' was on a return voyage to Nassau when they sighted a French ship. Captain Vane refused to board her. Rackman instigated a mutiny and took over the ship, forcing Vane to walk the plank and declaring himself as Captain. He renamed the ship the 'Adventure' and became known throughout the region as Calico Jack for the breeches and shirt of white calico that he always wore. Nassau had become the refuge of a great many cut-throat pirates through an amnesty that had been decreed by the Governor. It was inevitable that Anne would find her way to the waterfront where these vicious drunken louts dwelt.

Her best friends were the pirates' paramours and a notorious homosexual named Pierre who ran a ladies establishment on the island. It was through his connection that she met Chidley Bayard, one of the richest men in the Caribbean. She had to dispose of Chidley's current companion, a Spanish beauty named Maria Vargas, which she did in a fight to the death. She accompanied Chidley on many of his business trips to Jamaica, but on one occasion she slugged the sister-in-law of the Governor in the mouth and was hauled off to jail. Bayard managed to get her freed but refused to allow her to accompany him again. With Chidley away for much of the time, Anne soon discovered the type of real men that she had missed. And in particular Calico Jack.

The Kantaberry Tales

Theirs was a mutual attraction, a partnership fashioned in heaven, a meeting of two passionate personalities, frightening in its intensity. They were inseparable; and as if by divine intervention Anne's husband Jimmy was lost at sea in a hurricane, conveniently removing the one final barrier from the two lovers union. When Calico Jack went back to sea, Anne went with him. She dressed as a man, and as the scruffy members of Jack's crew would confirm when asked, she was as ruthless as the best of them and more proficient with her sword and dagger than even Jack himself. She was fearless in battle and delighted in torturing the defeated merchants of the ransacked ships. Two months after they went to sea Anne discovered that she was pregnant. She was dismayed at the prospect of motherhood and pleaded with Jack to keep her condition a secret. She stayed on the ship until her sixth month but then went ashore to await the birth. Once ashore she began to look forward to the baby's arrival, even hoping that she might have a girl, a sign that just maybe she was ready to settle down. Her little girl arrived two months premature and died within an hour of her birth.

Anne was convinced that she had caused the baby's demise and was inconsolable. She wept bitter tears for days after the tragedy and seemed to have lost her will to live. When Jack returned to retrieve his lady, he too was devastated by the loss but was unprepared for the state in which he found Anne. He gathered her few belongings and despite her protests took her aboard the 'Adventure' where, with just three trustworthy crew members, he set sail for the tranquil harbor of Ryal Island.

It was there, away from the temptations of New Providence that Jack nursed Anne back to health with a diet of fresh fish and the juice from the fruit of the kantaberry bushes which grew profusely on the island. The protected anchorage of Ryal Island afforded them the respite they both needed and they spent many days relaxing on board or trekking through the scrub land of this peaceful place. They discovered a series of natural shallow wells in the limestone rock which contained sweet fresh water, and it was here at the western end of the bay that they constructed a small shack. On two occasions they made the difficult passage past Spanish Wells and then on to Briland to visit Dunmore Town. They disguised themselves as a wealthy merchant and his wife to avoid any recognition from the local constabulary. There was a price on Jack's head for burning a large portion of the town to the ground during one of his many raids there. They secretly purchased provisions and on one trip they ventured into Saint Mary's church and were married by the Reverend Thompson.

They returned to Ryal and spent many weeks together as husband and wife. Anne discovered that she was pregnant once again and Jack decided that this time the baby would not be born in Nassau. They sailed for Kingston, Jamaica, where they thought that they would find a kindlier reception than the one they knew they would receive in Nassau. They had both made enemies in Nassau and it was possible that they were both wanted criminals. Eight days out of Kingston the 'Adventure' was overtaken by a King's vessel, subjected to cannon fire and boarded. Jack and his drunken crew were quickly overpowered; only Anne offered any true resistance. They were clapped in irons and transported to Jamaica as prisoners.

Calico Jack and his crew were tried on November 16, 1720, before Sir Nicholas Laws. Despite his pleas of innocence and his promise of repentance, Jack was not spared and was hanged at Gallows Point later that same year.

Anne spoke at her own trial, pleading her condition as a defense to her execution. She received a stay of execution and was dispatched to the dungeons of Kingston until after the birth of her baby.

Word of Anne's confinement finally reached her Father and through his connections with the Governor she was secretly removed from the dungeons and deported back to South Carolina. Her baby boy was born on April 21, 1721, and was named John Cormac Rackman.

Anne, who was still only twenty years of age, and her son traveled to Virginia where she married Joseph Burleigh, a longtime friend of her Father's. After giving birth to eight more children she died at the age of seventy-six and was buried in Sweetwater, Virginia.

Yvonne Provost could not remember a time in her life when she had been so happy. She had met a man who loved her, a man who was tender and considerate who treated her with respect and affection, two qualities that she had never known in any other man. Now as she swam leisurely in the calm warm waters along the shore of Royal Island, she gazed wondrously at the little coloured fish that made this coast their home and thought how perfect her life had become. She wore a snorkel mask on her face and flippers on her feet and a handkerchief sized bikini bottom that barely covered her. She was the colour of creamy coffee, single cream not double; the colour complimented her raven black hair making her look like a native as she slowly paddled through the shallow water. She stood up and as she did the water ran down her body causing it to glisten voluptuously in the sunshine. She waved at Johnnie.

Johnnie too was happier than he could ever remember. He waved back at Yvonne and said a silent prayer to whomever it was that had sent this beautiful girl into his life. She had fulfilled his every dream and desire. She was carefree in her attitude but could be serious when they talked about their future together. She was generous by nature and sexually insatiable. She was spontaneous in her actions and always ready to participate in any adventure. Johnnie had grown to love her and could not imagine a life without her. Now as he saw her half-naked in the shallow water, waving to him to join her, he downed the tools that he was using to fix the solar panel, and dove into the water to join her.

Two dolphins could not have been any more at home in the water than Yvonne and Johnnie. They cavorted together without effort, diving down to kiss each other while underwater, then rising up wrapped together as close as Siamese twins. One moment Yvonne was on his shoulders and the next she was between his legs, twisting and turning as she teased him with her naked body. The passionate love-making under the hot sun, which became the inevitable conclusion to their playtime, was one of their most satisfying events. It had become their daily routine.

Royal Island is presently privately owned by a family living in Florida. In 1929 this family began buying the many deeds to the five hundred and ten acres of land that had been owned by local families and their descendents. Eventually the family owned all the property and in 1938 constructed a unique mansion with paved roads, docks, caretaker's facilities, lavish gardens and sufficient bedrooms to accommodate twenty guests. The island has three, twenty foot deep, hand-hewn wells, and a fresh water pond is located in the central area of the main island. Since 1972, a date that happens to coincide with the advent of the Bahamas Independence from the British crown, the property has fallen into a state of disrepair. Two major hurricanes and many vandals have accounted for a continuation of this deterioration and today the buildings, roads and docks are either overgrown with vegetation or broken down. It is still possible to walk along the pathways that connect the docks on the south to those on the north shore. The road that circles the bay to the south-west is still recognizable as a road and with some care it can be followed almost to 'The Papps'. These are the two 'high' peaks that can be seen from eight to ten miles distant, and are usually the first land sighting when approaching from the north.

Johnnie and Yvonne spent many days exploring the remains of the mansion and its outbuildings. They followed the pathways around the island and visited the harbor on the north shore. From here they could see the curve of the north shore all the way to nearby Russell Island. It was after a day on this north coast, a day Johnnie had spent spear fishing around the numerous coral heads within easy swimming distance, that he returned to 'Soleil' with sufficient fish to feed them for the next few days, to find Yvonne studying the land to the south through their binoculars. She had a nautical chart under her arm which she referred to periodically as she continued to scrutinize the landscape. She barely acknowledged Johnnie as he climbed aboard with the fish.

"What are you looking at?" he asked.

"Those hills," she replied with a nod towards the 'Papps'.

"What's so special about them?"

"That old map you have. It's them."

"You lost me."

"You know, that old piece of a map you received from your great grandmother. It's a map of this part of the island."

"Why do you think that?"

Yvonne spread the chart on the deck and extracted the old map from the pocket of her shorts. She turned the old map so that it corresponded to the area of the chart that showed the elevation of the two peaks.

"See, those two marks represent the two peaks, and that line intersects a point on the mainland of Eleuthera known as Current Cut. I bet that you can see Current Cut from up there on a clear day."

Johnnie followed her reasoning and confirmed her findings.

"The name Ryall, could easily be Royal," he conjectured.

"Of course," she agreed enthusiastically. "Let's climb up there."

"We'll need a machete to cut through the bush".

"OK. Come on."

"Wait a minute. We'll need our shoes and long pants to protect our legs from the thorns of the kantaberry bushes."

They dressed in their 'winter' clothes, applied a liberal coating of bug repellent to any exposed skin, packed a small carry-bag with water, the machete, a box of crackers and the binoculars and paddled their dinghy across to the western end of the bay. The water shallowed to less than a foot in depth as they approached the shore where they dragged their boat onto the beach.

Johnnie led the way, hacking a pathway through the dense bush. Although the elevation of the 'Papps' is only seventy five to a hundred feet above sea level and they are only sixty yards from shore, it took the young couple all day to reach them. They took turns with the machete, both of them had blisters on their hands from the unaccustomed work and both were bitten by mosquitoes and red ants, but they finally arrived at the highest point of land on Royal Island.

Even without the binoculars it was easy to see the main coast of Eleuthera and the gap between Eleuthera and Current Island. While Yvonne was eating the last of the crackers, Johnnie studied the fragment of his old map. From the high point where they were now standing, and in the direction of the gap between the two islands they could see in the distance, the map showed two numbers. 139 and 16.

"You looked puzzled," said Yvonne as she looked at Johnnie's face.

"We're here," he said as he indicated a spot on the old map.

"What's the direction of the gap between those islands?"

Johnnie found his pocket compass and sighted it towards the gap.

"140," he said excitedly "That must be the 139 on the map. Now we have to figure out what the 16 means."

"Could be leagues to the water down there," Yvonne suggested.

"Or the miles to Current Cut."

"It's not that far. It must indicate a well or a cave on the bearing of 139."

"Sixteen paces? Sixteen yards? Sixteen feet? Take your pick".

"Let's cut a path along the sight line and see what we find," said Yvonne.

Slowly foot by foot they hacked their way through the bush. Johnnie checked every few feet with his pocket compass to make sure they were on line. On this downward slope the bush was far denser than it had been lower down and their progress was considerably slower. They were also extremely tired, hungry and thirsty, with only the juice from a few kantaberries to refresh them, but they carried on.

They reached a spot which they estimated to be sixteen feet from the apex of the 'Papps'; they cleared an area and searched the ground for a clue or something that would indicate that the maker of the map had concealed treasure or valuables in this place. But the ground was hard with no indication of a secret hiding place.

"Let's go back to the boat," said Johnnie "we're too tired. We'll come back tomorrow when we're fresh."

They retraced their steps along the trail they had carved out of the bush, threw their gear into the dinghy and rowed back to 'Soleil'. They prepared a quick meal before collapsing into bed. For the first time since they had set sail, they did not make love.

Early the following morning they awoke with new energy, ready to return to the bush and to proceed with their search. The sun was only an hour from sunrise as they once again looked out at the panoramic view of the surrounding islands from the top of Royal Island. With new vigor they commenced clearing the vegetation from the pathway that followed the 139 degree bearing. They had cleared a distance of about thirty five feet, or in their estimation sixteen paces, when the limestone rock at their feet revealed a crevice about four feet wide and two feet deep. There were many loose rocks in the crevice and they quickly removed them to discover a narrow opening to what appeared to be a well or a cave. With the machete and their bare hands they removed more rocks that had fallen into the hole, until they could see into the little cave. It was empty. There was no chest full of doubloons, no hoard of pirate treasure, nothing that would make them rich for the rest of their lives.

"Why would someone have gone to all the trouble of making a map of this location if there's nothing there?" posed Yvonne with obvious disappointment in her voice.

"I dunno," replied Johnnie from the brink of the little cave. He was laying full-length on the ground at the edge of the cave with his head deep into the opening.

"I think I can see water at the bottom. Hold my feet, I'm going in."

As Yvonne held on grimly to his feet, Johnnie slowly slid his shoulders then his upper body into the cave. He found an old bottle. He backed out with the bottle in his hands.

"That's all?" asked Yvonne.

"Fraid so. Nothing but a bottle. It could be valuable," he said hopefully.

They returned to their boat with the bottle which they sat in a place of honour on the cockpit table. After a quick breakfast, Johnnie picked up the bottle in his hands and examined it more carefully.

"It looks old. Probably a brandy bottle," he said out loud.

"Too bad there's no brandy inside" commented Yvonne from inside the cabin.

As Johnnie turned the bottle around in his hands he noticed something inside that seem to move as he turned the bottle end up. The dark brown coloured glass was so thick and opaque that it was impossible to see into the inside. He removed the stopper, turned the bottle over and shook out its contents. A tightly rolled up sheet of parchment slid out from the bottle.

"Yvonne," he called "I've found something."

With Yvonne peering anxiously over his shoulder, Johnnie unrolled the paper. He read the flamboyant writing that filled one side of what was obviously an official document.

"It's a marriage certificate," he said incredulously, "between Anne Cormac and John Rackman!"

For the moment the significance of this discovery was lost on them both. But later in their life together they came to realize that Anne Cormac was a very distant relation to Johnnie and her marriage to Calico Jack legitimized the birth of his dubious ancestor and allowed him to claim a part of the family's fortune that had been previously denied to him.

As Johnnie always explained to his close friends whenever he was asked, "A lot of people assumed that my family was a bunch of stupid bastards. At least now I can honestly say that they're not; bastards that is!"

VOODOO

On Thursday April 10th 2003, the government of Haiti officially sanctioned voodoo as a religion, allowing practitioners to begin performing ceremonies from baptisms to marriages with legal authority. Many who practice voodoo praised the move, but said much needs to be done to make up for the centuries of ridicule and persecution in Haiti and some other Caribbean countries where the practice of voodoo has been banned.

President Jean-Bertrand Aristide invited voodoo adherents and organizations to register with the Ministry of Religious Affairs. Aristide, a former Roman Catholic priest, said that he recognizes voodoo as a religion like any other. 'It is an essential part of our national identity', he was quoted as saying' and its institutions represent a considerable portion of Haiti's 8.3 million people.

Voodoo practitioners believe in a supreme God and spirits who link the human with the divine. The spirits can be summoned by offerings that include everything from rum to roosters.

Voodoo is an inseparable part of Haitian art, literature, music and film. Hymns are played on the radio and voodoo ceremonies are broadcast on television along with Christian services. For centuries voodoo has been looked down upon as little more than superstition, and at times has been the victim of ferocious persecution. A campaign led by the Catholic Church in the 1940's led to the destruction of voodoo temples and sacred voodoo objects.

Within the voodoo society, there are no accidents. Practitioners believe that nothing, and no event, has a life of its own. That is why 'vous deux', (voo doo) becomes you two, or you too. The universe is all one. Each thing affects something else. Nature knows it. Many spiritualists agree that we are not separate; we all serve as parts of One. So, in essence, what you do unto another, you do unto you, because you are the other. Voo doo. View you. We are the mirrors of each other's soul. God is manifest through the spirits of ancestors who can bring good or harm and must be honored in ceremonies. There is a sacred cycle between the living and the dead.

The Kantaberry Tales

If he was anything, Fergus Pinder of Spanish Wells was a creature of habit. From the clothes he wore to the food he consumed he was predictable and proud of it. He liked what he liked and was quick to correct anyone who had the nerve to argue with him. He was always right. He got up at the same time every morning and went to bed at the exact same time every evening. No matter what. He ate boiled fish every Wednesday, fried chicken every Friday and for dessert he always had a slice of kantaberry pie. He had never tasted any of the new fangled foods that they sold at Food Fair. His usual comment, when he was asked about a new fad or a scientific breakthrough, was 'it's a load of rubbish'. Now, after twenty years on a fishing boat, he worked as an auto mechanic and with each new model of car that came to his shop for repair, he delighted in telling the proud owner that in his opinion, 'it was a load of rubbish'. You couldn't beat a good old Ford. Black was his favorite colour for a car. 'You can't beat black,' he would say as he worked on a new yellow Toyota, 'why would anyone buy a piece of yellow rubbish such as this?'

He attended the People's Church every Sunday morning and Wednesday evening, as long as he could be home and in bed by his usual hour. In the nearly forty years that he had attended church, he had always worn the same colour suit, black, the same colour tie and shoes, black, and the same white shirt. 'Why would I wear a blue shirt,' he would say to his wife when she mistakenly questioned his taste in clothes. In his own mind he was a good Christian, and in many ways he was. He didn't drink, smoke or take drugs. He prayed every day, he read a verse or two from the Bible at least once a day, he was generous with his support of his Church, he was honest in his daily life and he never told a lie or even thought an evil thought. For want of a better expression, one might call him a 'selective' Christian. We all know the type. They go to extreme lengths to defend their belief in God and Jesus, and will quote verbatim, verses from the Bible that they interpret as confirmation of their particular beliefs. If they look long and hard enough, they will find words in the Bible that can be twisted into defending, racism, alcoholism, narcissism and condemning homosexuality.

It was difficult to refer to Fergus as prejudicial. He had never thought about prejudice for long enough to make a prejudicial assessment. To him it was an easy matter to decide if a person was worthy, and if they happened to be Haitian, Black, or Hispanic, from Europe, Canada or the United States it was of no consequence to him. He could detect unworthiness among his white neighbors too, be they Sweetings, Aubreys, Newbolds or even Pinders. He suffered from the 'Archie Bunker' complex; if you're not like me, you're unworthy.

But for all his faults, of which he was not aware, he was a 'good' man. He worked hard, and in his own manner, he cared and supported his family. He had three daughters. The youngest of them worked in the office of the garage, where she answered the phone, kept track of the daily purchases of oil and gas, ordered supplies as they were needed and made the coffee. Or, in Fergus's case, tea. He didn't drink coffee. His other daughters also lived at home with him and his wife, none were married but one did have a small child. 'A gift from the Lord' was the way in which Fergus had defended the illegitimate birth. His wife was a weak-willed woman who had learned to tolerate her husband's bigoted outlook on life and had, a long time ago, decided that passivity was the best policy. Now, after almost thirty years of marriage to the man, she had developed a streak of independence. She had been forced to become deceptive in her actions because of his intolerance. She had discovered, purely by accident, that she had occult powers. She could predict the weather better than any meteorologist, she could determine where the best fishing could be had, and she could tell fortunes. She read Tarot Cards, tea leaves or astrological signs and she was never wrong in her predictions. She would gaze in secret into her crystal ball and tell her neighbors what they wanted to hear. Her talent made her feel important for the first time in her life and she now had more friends in the community than she had had at any time since she'd left school. Fergus knew something of her activity but had dismissed it as 'a load of rubbish' and had not considered it of sufficient importance to cause a domestic disturbance.

"What harm could there be in it," he conjectured. He searched and found a short passage in his Bible that showed that King David had made predictions by the stars, thus proving to himself that his wife's actions were adequately condoned.

Fergus always drank freshly brewed tea in the morning with his breakfast. He always had two cups. The tea had to be brewed using tea leaves, not tea bags, and most importantly it had to be hot.

Monday mornings at the Pinder household were always hectic. With five adults and a baby to feed, it was surprising that breakfast was prepared at all, but Mrs. Pinder was a whiz in the kitchen and all the members of the family were fed their favorite foods and hustled out of the house within thirty minutes. Fergus was the last to leave on this particular Monday morning and before he hurried out the door he swallowed the remaining inch of tea from his cup. It was only luke warm and he grimaced as he threw the contents of the cup down his throat. There had been tea leaves at the bottom of the cup.

"Can't you do anything right?" he berated his wife. He spat the tea leaves back into the cup and stalked out the door to work. He was still grumbling as he drove the few blocks to the garage. He had a brake job to do on a Ford pickup, his kind of truck, even though it was white not black. Without interruptions he figured he'd have the truck completed by lunchtime, but if he didn't he planned to work through the lunch hour in order to finish the job. He had told his wife not to expect him home for lunch, and he had instructed his daughter in the office not to call him to the phone unless it was a dire emergency.

He derived great satisfaction from his work, he liked the smell of oil and grease and, even though he rarely participated in them, he enjoyed listening to the conversations of his fellow workers. He was always ready to correct them if they were off base, but for the most part he held his tongue diplomatically.

He was engrossed in the brake job, humming quietly to himself, when his daughter called.

"Daddy. It's for you!"

"Who is it?" he yelled back. "I told you I didn't want to be disturbed."

"It's Mummy."

"Tell her I'll call her back."

"She says it's important."

Derek Hawkins

He was fit to be tied. What could be so important? He grabbed a rag to wipe his greasy hands as he entered the small office to answer the phone.

"This better be important," he snarled into the receiver.

He waited for a moment for his wife to answer. She didn't say anything.

"Well," he shouted, "what is it?"

"It's the leaves," she said nervously.

"Leaves," he screamed. "What leaves?"

"The ones in the cup. The ones you spat out."

"The what?"

"The tea leaves you spat into your cup as you were leaving. They made a pattern!"

He took a moment to count to ten before he was calm enough to respond.

"You called me here, dragged me away from an important job to tell me that the tea leaves that I spat out formed a pattern. You must think that I'm as crazy as you are."

"It's a sign," she interrupted dramatically.

"A sign, eh? A sign that you've lost your mind no doubt!"

"It's a circle with a line through it. It's an omen. It means death. Actually a sacrifice," she stated.

"It's a load of rubbish. That's what it is."

"I'm taking the girls and our granddaughter away with me to somewhere safe. Someone is going to die. You can come with us, but if you don't we'll be gone when you get home."

Then she hung up.

Fergus went back to his work without another thought about the leaves and the impending danger.

His youngest daughter was ready to leave for lunch and he asked her to make him a cup of tea before she left. He would work through lunch to finish.

She placed the freshly made tea next to his bench before she went home.

Fergus forgot about the tea until he came out from under the car to find a wrench. The tea was almost cold by then but he drank it down in one gulp to quench his thirst. He received another mouthful of tea leaves in his mouth and spat them back into the empty cup. An inexplicable force drew his eyes to the contents of the cup.

Derek Hawkins

The colour drained from his face and his legs became weak as he looked at the circular pattern of leaves with a jagged line through it, which had formed inside the china cup. He was dumbfounded and scared at what he saw. He didn't want to admit to or acknowledge the presence of the omen, but as he looked into the cup once again, he knew that his wife had been correct. This was a warning. A warning of impending doom. He called home, but there was no answer.

He drove like a mad-man all the way home, nearly running down two of his neighbors as he sped by them. Their faces reflected their surprise at seeing the usually placid Fergus, speeding through town. He leapt out of the car almost before it had stopped and ran to his front door. He fumbled for his key and finally flung the door open. There was nobody home. No wife, no daughters, no granddaughter and no pets. Everything was quiet. Fergus felt certain that some disaster was about to strike him as he searched every room looking for his family. He began to panic. There was an eerie feeling about the house, a sense that something supernatural was about to happen. Fergus fell to the floor in a daze. He knew that his time had come and that he was totally powerless.

He drew his knees up under his chin in a fetal position and waited.

The phone rang. Its high pitched ring made him jump.

"I'm so glad that you're home," said his wife. "It's too bad that you were too late to be with us. But don't worry, I think there's still time for me to help you."

"Please help me," he pleaded. "You don't know what happened at the garage. I spat out another omen!"

"I know, I know."

"You do?"

"Of course I do. Now you must do exactly as I tell you, and do it quickly. You don't have much time!"

"I'm listening,"

"Go to the fridge and take out the chicken that's defrosting for tonight's dinner. Take the long carving knife and plunge it through the chicken. Let the blood run out on the floor, it doesn't matter if it soils your black shoes. Next get the string from the kitchen drawer and make a loop large enough to go over your head. Tie each of the chicken's legs to one end of the string and put the loop over your head, so that the chicken hangs level with your heart. Next, look in the bottom drawer of the cabinet next to the washing machine and you will find a large roll of bright red wrapping paper. Cut a three foot circle of the paper and place it at the foot of the stairs. Now stand in the circle with the chicken hanging around your neck and wait until I get home. I should be there in twenty minutes. Oh, I almost forgot, you must take off all your clothes."

Fergus did exactly as he had been told. He felt a little self-conscious standing naked on the red paper, but he was more than willing to follow the instructions if it meant avoiding the sacrifice. And he waited.

He heard a car. It must be his wife. Then another car, and then another. He heard footsteps coming to the front door. The door burst open and in walked his wife, his three daughters, his granddaughter, four of his friends from the garage and their wives all chanting "Happy Birthday you old Fool."

It took three weeks for the news of his birthday surprise to subside. His reputation had not been compromised; in fact, he began to see himself as others saw him, and this observation changed his personality. He purchased a new red truck, a new brown suit, a gold chain to hang around his neck, and for breakfast he replaced his tea with a glass of kantaberry juice.

Mrs. Pinder's reputation increased dramatically as her services became more and more in demand from the local people. On Saturday nights she could be found on Russell Island attending the cock fights with her three daughter's boy friends. She used her crystal ball to predict the winning birds in each event and was often seen painting occult signs on the favorite roosters with blood from the previous bout's loser.

Many members of the Haitian community referred to her as the High Priestess and held her in high regard. They would sing songs of praise to her and chant her name when they attended their voodoo services on Russell Island.

Fergus wasn't convinced of his wife's power until she correctly predicted the winners of the Super Bowl and the Kentucky Derby. As his business increased in popularity, from the number of Haitians who sought him out to fix their vehicles, his attitude towards them changed. He became more human, less predictable and a better Christian.

It was also rumoured that the substantial increase in the family's spending power was attributable to Fergus having a little friendly flutter on a horse or two. But it's just a rumour.

TWO TEENS

Cassie.

Cassie was just two months shy of her sixteenth birthday when she missed her period. She prayed that there was some explanation other than the obvious one. She waited for a month, then missed again.

It was a secret that she knew she couldn't keep. Sooner or later she knew that she would have to tell her mother and her boyfriend. But she had to be certain.

To buy a pregnancy test kit at the pharmacy was out of the question. Everyone would hear about it. She would have to find a way to buy one in Harbour Island, but this would entail a trip on the Fast Ferry and she knew that there was no way that she could make such a trip on her own without raising her family's suspicions. She could confide in her boyfriend and ask him to make the trip, but he was away fishing and wasn't expected back for another ten days.

Her girlfriend's older sister was expecting a baby in a few months and it was quite possible that she would have a test kit at her home. Cassie decided to casually drop in to see her girlfriend, find an excuse to use the bathroom and check the medicine cabinet for a kit. She walked the two blocks to Diana's house and was lucky to find her friend in the front yard. She was invited in for a soda.

"Is something wrong?" asked Diana.

"I don't feel well. Can I use the bathroom?"

She locked the door and began searching through the medicine cabinet. There was no test kit. She looked in the cupboard under the counter and there it was. A box named First Response. How appropriate, she thought. She read the instructions carefully; she could not afford to make a mistake in a matter as critical as this. She sat on the toilet and held the strip in the stream of her urine. She waited for the subscribed time. It was positive. She was definitely pregnant!

Cassie wasn't shocked by the result. She'd been sure of her condition, so the test was nothing more than confirmation. She looked at herself in the bathroom mirror, trying to determine if her belly had grown at all. She pulled her shirt tight across her body and examined her profile. There was no change. Nobody could tell.

She didn't look any different, but she felt different. Not physically, but mentally. She was going to have a baby. The enormity of those simple words began to have a profound effect on her. She wasn't ashamed, nor was she scared. She had many friends who had had babies as young as she was and they had survived just fine. Her own mother was still quite young, and she was happy enough. The more she thought about her situation the better she felt. She could take care of a baby as well as anybody; it's what she'd always wanted, to be a mother, to have a good husband, a nice home and her friends.

She came out of the bathroom with her head held high.

"Are you OK?" Diana asked.

"Couldn't be better. I'm pregnant," she announced.

By the time she left Diana's home she had sworn her friend to secrecy, "At least until I've had a chance to tell Mummy and Chad," she had explained. Chad was the father.

Chad was twenty two. He worked as a fisherman on the 'Blue Horizon' with his Daddy and his brother. He had been fishing for seven years and during that time he had earned more than three hundred thousand dollars, tax free and without any deductions. His only extravagance had been the purchase of a new bright blue pickup truck with an awesome sound system that jarred the fillings out of the teeth of those unfortunate enough to be within fifty yards of him as he passed by. He'd known Cassie all of her short life and knew that she was easy. Having children was not on his list of priorities.

Telling her Mummy the news was not as hard as Cassie had imagined it would be. After the initial shock had worn off, her Mummy had given her a reassuring hug and told her not to worry. She was concerned about her daughter's health and had insisted that she visit the doctor and also start a diet that included plenty of fresh foods and a daily intake of kantaberries. "No more fries for you, my girl," she had said.

Unplanned teenage pregnancy is uncommon in Spanish Wells. The strong influence of the church and the importance of family have instilled a high moral value into the younger members of the community, much higher than those found in most other communities within the Bahamas. The words abortion or termination are just words. Neither would be given any consideration. It became apparent to Cassie that while she was ecstatic about her pregnancy, her feeling of joy was not being shared by her friends or any members of her family other than her mother. Groups of shoppers would stop talking when she approached; several of her class mates openly shunned her and her phone had stopped ringing. She was being treated as an outcast. Hers was not the behavior that the women on the island condoned, nor did they want her influencing their offspring.

The doctor's visit was a nightmare. Apart from the fact that she had to submit to an embarrassing examination, the waiting room was full and all eyes were directed towards her. If she had had any doubts before the visit about her condition or her status in the town, both were now confirmed.

"Everybody hates me," she sobbed to her mother. "They think I'm a slut."

"Don't be silly. Of course they don't."

"They do. I can see it in their eyes."

"You mustn't let a few narrow-minded old biddies upset you. You've got to stay happy. The baby needs a happy mother," her mother consoled her.

"It's my friends too," she cried.

Her tears would not stop. She lay in bed and sobbed for the rest of the day until she finally fell asleep.

She left the house early the following morning and rode her bicycle to the beach. She needed to be alone to think about what she had done and what her future held. The beach was deserted. She kicked off her shoes, felt the sand between her toes and walked into the water until her knees were covered. She hoisted the skirt of her cotton dress up to her waist and walked further into deeper water. The water felt cold to her warm thighs, but she walked on allowing the water to rise higher and higher until it was up to her waist. She wondered if her baby could sense the presence of the water or if the water could somehow miraculously cleanse her of the guilt that she now felt. She remained in the water until her feet sank deep into the sand and she lost control over them. She wondered if she stayed in the water all day whether she would continue to sink lower and lower into the sand. Nobody would care, she thought.

She knew that Chad would be home the next day and that he would hear the news from one of the gossipy neighbors. Although she referred to Chad as her 'boyfriend', he was really nothing more than a casual friend and she had no doubt in her mind as to what his reaction to the news would be. She wished that he felt the same way about her as she felt about him, but he never had. She had practically thrown herself at him in an attempt to prove to her girl friends that she could win him for herself. He was the coolest guy on the island and was idolized by most of the fifteen and sixteen year old girls. For a while she had been the envy of her friends, but now she was the brunt of their jokes.

He had never dated her in the true sense of the word. She had been available to ride in his truck with him and his friends whenever he had wanted her. They were seldom alone.

She'd worn a top that she had 'borrowed' from her mother, it was gold coloured with sparkles across the front. It made her tiny breasts appear larger than they were which was why she wore it. They met at the Gap. It was not an arranged meeting; the Gap was the place where they all congregated, and she knew he would be there. There were four of them in his truck. They drove around for a while, stopped at Eagle's Landing to shoot pool and to have snack, and then Chad drove his two friends home. She sat in the front seat with him for the first time and moved over to be close to him. His hand slipped around her shoulder as if by accident and his fingers touched her breast. She felt her legs weaken as the truck slowed to the side of the road by the bridge. He drove over the grass until the truck was hidden among the trees and the kantaberry bushes.

It all happened so quickly. Neither of them spoke. There was no foreplay, no tenderness in his actions, no romantic whispers in her ear. Just sex. Consensual sex.

Cassie just hoped that he would at least remember her name. She also came to know that he told his friends about their exploits because one of them had made dirty insinuations about her to her face. She had blushed and denied the accusations, but she had felt used and betrayed.

The tide had risen while she had contemplated her future and relived her past. She had two options. She had to hope that Chad would be honorable and marry her, or she could raise the baby on her own as a single mother. She was sure that her mother would support her but was it fair to expect her parents to make such a sacrifice? She knew that they had plans to travel when she left; they had often talked about their plans and joked with her about her leaving. Her father had sent her a humorous birthday card last year in which he had written 'only five more years'. The message was meant to be funny but there was an underlying truth behind it. If Chad refused to take the responsibility she knew she would be devastated.

She dragged her feet from the sand and waded back to the beach. Would a life with Chad be everything she hoped it would be? If he married her for the sake of the baby, could she endure a life knowing that he not only didn't love her, but that he also resented her? It was a choice between two evils. The options were depressing and any joy that she had felt with the discovery of her pregnancy had now been overshadowed by depression and uncertainty. She ambled sadly along the beach on the verge of tears. Her short life had been changed forever by a stupid mistake. She wished that she could cancel out the events of the night that she had spent with Chad, but she couldn't; the evidence was right there inside her.

Her eyes were red from all the crying and when she arrived home she ran upstairs to avoid her mother's questions. Her mother followed her and after knocking gently on the bedroom door, she tip-toed in to see her daughter. She didn't like what she saw.

"What's the matter, honey?" she asked as she noticed the red eyes and the sad expression.

"I've messed up everybody's lives," she sobbed, "mine, yours and Daddy's."

"That's not true. I'm looking forward to having a new baby to care for."

"It's not fair. You shouldn't have to suffer because of me."

Her mother hugged her tightly to comfort her.

"Chad's boat's back. He's coming over later to talk to your Daddy," she said.

"So he knows? Somebody told him?"

"Yes," she replied.

She was still in her bedroom when she heard Chad's truck drive up. She watched from her window and saw him step out of the cab, throw his cigarette into the bushes, comb through his hair with his fingers and walk to the front door. He was here to see her Daddy, not her.

She had been told to stay out of the way in her bedroom while the men talked. She was not to come down unless Chad asked to see her. He didn't. He was only in the house for a few minutes. She watched from her window as he departed. She went downstairs to find out what he had said. Both her Mummy and Daddy looked distraught as they sat together on the sofa. They never looked at her as she came to sit across from them. It was her Daddy who broke the silence.

"He said that there's no proof that it's his."

Cassie began to cry again.

"He said it could belong to anyone of a dozen other boys around town."

Cassie became hysterical and began to scream.

Her mother hugged her.

"Tell me it isn't true Cassie," demanded her father.

She never answered.

The next day she rode her bicycle to the beach again. She removed her shoes as she had done on her previous visit, pushed her toes into the sand, and without hiking up her skirt she walked out into the water. This time she didn't stop when the water reached her waist.

Her body washed ashore later in the day on the incoming tide.

Ritchie.

When he was six years old his uncle bought him a guitar for his birthday. It had four strings, a bridge and a carrying case. By the time he was seven he could play the National Anthem, three hymns, Jingle Bells and the first few bars of Greensleeves. When he went to Sunday school at seven, he discovered the piano. He learned to play it in less than six months.

Derek Hawkins

Ritchie Sweeting was a child prodigy.

The only piano teacher in Spanish Wells was a retired American lady who lived on Russell Island. Ritchie's mother had never met the lady formally but had seen her around town on several occasions. She decided to take her son with her when she went to ask the lady whether she would consider giving Ritchie piano lessons. She was hoping that she wouldn't charge too much.

"How old is your son?" the teacher asked.

"I'm eight," Ritchie answered immediately.

Claire Richardson was taken aback by the boy's boldness. He certainly seemed to be confident and self-assured, more so than other eight year olds she had taught.

"I'd like to hear you play something," Claire suggested.

The piano that Claire owned was a baby grand, a much better instrument than the one Ritchie had learned to play on at the church. He sat on the stool, adjusted its height with the knob on its side and played a warm-up scale. He liked what he heard; the notes were far easier to push than those on the older piano.

"What can you play?" Claire asked. She was expecting him to play a simple lullaby or a familiar song.

"I'll play Chopin's Fantasie-Impromptu in C-sharp minor," he said matter-of-factly.

Claire raised her eyes and looked at Ritchie's Mother in doubt.

The eight year old closed his eyes for a moment to collect his thoughts, and then he played this very difficult masterpiece flawlessly. He ended with a flourish and remained seated at the piano.

Claire was speechless. She could not believe what she had just heard.

"Is something wrong?" asked Mrs. Sweeting after a long silence descended over the room.

Claire ignored Ritchie's Mother, recaptured her composure and directed her questions directly to the boy.

"Can you read music?"

"No."

"Can you play everything that you hear?"

"Yes." he replied.

"Have you ever heard the recordings of any of the great masters? Rubenstein, Horowitz or Emanuel Ax?"

"No. But my Daddy has a Yanni CD!"

Claire shook her head in disbelief. The boy had incredible talent but little or no musical appreciation.

"Will you give him piano lessons?"

"It's not piano lessons that he needs. He needs to learn about music. Playing the piano is much more than hitting the correct notes. He can already do that. He needs to interpret the music, to play the notes with imagination and originality. I'll help him as best I can, but if he is to realize his potential and if he wants to become a true artist he will have to dedicate all of his time to studying. It could be very expensive."

For the next four years Ritchie spent all of his spare time at the home of Claire Richardson. His bicycle tires wore a groove in the roadway from his house to hers. 'If I don't make it as a pianist'" he thought, "I'll enter the Tour de France."

Claire taught him about music. She watched his facial expressions as he responded to the beauty of the music. She exposed him to the world of classical music through the recorded performances of the world's greatest musicians. He was inspired by what he heard and the level of his own piano playing soared to new heights as he responded to the challenge of the masters.

Claire's philosophy was simple. Since that first encounter, four years ago, she had known that he was a more accomplished piano player than she had ever been. and she knew that if he was to become a concert pianist he would need exposure to music. All kinds of music. She introduced him to operas, concertos, symphonies, chamber and choral music. He began to understand the meaning of interpretation, the difference between great and mediocre, and he also came to realize that even though he had natural talent, talent alone was not enough. Success required hard work and dedication. Ritchie was like a sponge, soaking up everything that was placed before him. His growth as a pianist and as a musician was nothing less than remarkable. It soon became obvious to Claire that he needed to move to another level of instruction. She had reached an impasse.

She decided to talk things over with Ritchie's parents on Sunday morning after church. She finagled an invitation to lunch that consisted of soused conch and rice followed with fresh baked kantaberry cookies. When lunch was over and before the football game started, she plunged ahead with her concerns about Ritchie's musical education.

"I have to talk to you both about your son's progress and what I think should be the next step. He's learned everything I can teach him. He needs a new teacher."

"I don't understand," said Ritchie's Father. "He's only eleven. Are you saying he knows more than you?"

"Not exactly, but his skills are of a far higher level than any other pupil I've ever taught. I'm not qualified to teach him. I'm beginning to hold him back."

"What should we do then?"

"He needs to study composition, harmony and structure, subjects that are beyond my expertise. He has to go abroad, to Europe or America."

Nobody commented for a moment. The impact of Claire's announcement had come as a shock. Ritchie's Father broke the silence.

"I read somewhere that Mozart was only seven or eight when he composed much of his music. You can't tell me that he studied composition or harmony."

Above all else, Claire did not want a confrontation with the family. She was trying to help in Ritchie's development, not create a division within the family, but she sensed an air of skepticism in the Father's tone.

It was Ritchie who answered his Father.

"There was only one Mozart, Daddy. He was a genius!"

"And you're not?"

"No, Daddy. I'm just gifted."

Ritchie's maturity always amazed Claire. His perception of a situation was uncanny for one so young. She listened in amazement as he tenderly lectured his poorly educated Father about his gift.

"Very few people are gifted," he began. "Why I am, and why my sister isn't, is a mystery. Last week I watched a concert by the Three Tenors from Miami, and during the intermission Luciano Pavarotti was interviewed. He was asked about his gift. His answer was very simple. 'It's a gift from God' he said 'and I am its receptacle. My voice belongs to God, he has entrusted its care to me. I look after it and I try to improve it. When I sing I share God's gift with those who choose to listen. For me not to sing would be a sin'.

Ritchie continued "I'm not suggesting that my talent is as great as his, but if I don't play up to my potential, it too would be a sin."

Ritchie's Father stole a look at Claire. He wanted to be sure that his son's speech had not been rehearsed for this occasion, but as he saw tears in her eyes, he knew that she too had been moved by Ritchie's simple assessment of his gift.

Ritchie's Mummy was in tears as she looked at her husband. Their eyes met and they both nodded in agreement.

"You know that we are not rich people," he said, "but we'll do whatever we can to further his development. I just hope that it'll be worth it."

Ritchie hugged both his parents. He nodded his head towards the television where the Miami Dolphin's game was just about to start, and said laughingly to his Daddy "The best concert pianist in the world doesn't earn as much money as that linebacker does!"

Claire told them about a world famous music teacher who had retired to Florida after teaching in New York for thirty-five years.

"He's taught the best," she said, "and even though he's retired he still has a couple of students. I've contacted him and he's agreed to listen to Ritchie play, but he's made no commitment to teach him. I have a small house in Coral Springs and Ritchie is welcome to live there with me."

"But what about school?"

"I'll tutor him for a while, but I'm hoping that he'll earn a scholarship to a good music school. His piano studies will take up most of his time, four or five hours every day."

The Kantaberry Tales

"You're giving up so much," said Ritchie's Mother.

"He's given me a new lease on life. I've not given anything up."

Ritchie and Claire flew to Fort Lauderdale three weeks later. On the first Saturday after their arrival, Claire purchased two tickets to the Broward Center for the Performing Arts where Maurizio Pollini was scheduled to perform with the Florida Philharmonic orchestra.

This was to be the first time that Ritchie would see and hear a live concert. He had listened to Claire's CDs and he was familiar with every bar of the Rachmaninoff Piano Concerto that Pollini would play, but when the music began on Saturday night he was simply overwhelmed. If he had any doubts before, they were all dispelled. He must learn to play like Pollini. It was all he could think about.

On Friday he had an audition with Heinrik Clausson the famous teacher. The audition was to be held in the teacher's home. Strangely, Ritchie was not nervous. Claire was.

Clausson was an old man who had a difficult time walking, which was why, he explained, that he sat most of the time. His eyes were alive and he reassured Claire and Ritchie that his hearing was as good as ever. He shook hands with Ritchie and thrust him in the direction of the piano.

"Play," he commanded.

Ritchie had chosen to play a prelude by Federico Mompou. He loved the simple haunting music of this rather obscure French composer for its combination of harmonies and subtle key changes. When he had finished playing, he sat at the piano and waited for the old teacher to say something.

"An unusual choice," the old man said.

Ninety-nine percent of the fresh new piano players that he auditioned chose to play works by Chopin or Beethoven.

"Tell me again how old are you?"

"I'm eleven."

"And why did you choose that particular piece?"

"Because I like it."

"But why? Don't you like Chopin or Beethoven?"

"Of course I do, but I come from a small island in the Bahamas where it's quiet and peaceful. The only sounds are those of the gulls and terns; Mompou's music fits my temperament."

"Eleven, eh," he mumbled. "You're a remarkable young man. I'd be honored to be your teacher."

Ritchie worked hard under the guidance of Heinrik Clausson for the next two years. Through Clausson's recommendation he was awarded a full scholarship to the Eastman School of Music in Rochester, New York, one of the most prestigious music schools in the country.

Two months shy of *his* sixteenth birthday he played his first concert with the New York Philharmonic.

BUGGIES

For the first time visitor to Spanish Wells or Harbour Island, the sight of golf carts being used as transportation comes as a bit of a shock. But when you think about it, it makes a lot of sense. They go forever on a tank of gas, or an overnight charge if they're electric, they are virtually maintenance free and relatively inexpensive. On both islands it's possible to rent a buggy, as they are called, for less than fifty dollars a day, and just like Hertz, they come with unlimited mileage. Most of them arrive in the Bahamas directly from golf courses in the United States. Either the course has gone out of business, or they've decided to switch from gas-powered to electric, or vice versa. On some rare occasions the golf club members decide that they want red carts instead of green and the green carts are disposed of. That was the case when fourteen green golf carts were purchased by Herman's Buggy Rentals. The carts were shipped from the golf course in Palm Beach by truck to Dania where they were transferred to a freighter for the trip to their destination of Harbour Island. Within one day of their arrival the green carts were in service, earning their owner Herman some much needed extra income. The carts came complete; some even had gas in the tank. Many had those little pencils that golfers use to mark their score cards, and all the carts came equipped with two plastic containers full of sand. The sand was intended to be used to fill divots.

Tony Casiano was not a good golfer. No matter how many lessons he took, no matter how often he changed clubs, balls, shirts, pants or shoes, he never broke a hundred. He was a member of the exclusive Winston Downs Country Club, a fancy club located just north of West Palm Beach on sixty acres of pristine waterfront property. He played golf whenever he was in town, which was only four or five times during the winter; no matter how hard he tried to juggle his busy schedule, he never seemed to be able to find more time to spend on the golf course. He loved to play. He was competitive by nature and golf presented him with an arena where he could display his individual toughness, but his business commitments interfered with his pleasure. He once figured out that each round of golf that he did manage to play at the club cost him over five thousand dollars. But then, money was no object to Tony.

In business he was ruthless, but in his personal life he was a pussycat. He wasted more money than other members of his family earned each year. For Tony, money was easy to come by and a necessary component of his life, allowing him to rub shoulders with people who ordinarily would not give him the time of day. But as hard as he tried to weasel his way into Palm Beach society, he knew that it was a lost cause. His tough exterior, his lack of formal education and his pushy ways formed a barrier to his acceptance.

There were two endearing features to his character. He was deeply concerned about children and he was also very superstitious. It was easy to understand the reason why he supported charities which were concerned with underprivileged kids, he had been one himself, but it was harder to understand why he was so superstitious. He was a fatalist. If he wore a red tie to a business meeting, and the meeting was unusually successful, he would wear a red tie every time he dealt with the same business people again. If he met a girl that seemed to enjoy his company, he would always remember the clothes that he wore, or the cologne that he used, and he would use them again on their next meeting. He left nothing to chance.

And so it was with golf.

Derek Hawkins

He would always remember Saturday, April 3rd; it was the day that he broke a hundred and lost only one ball. Everything came together, his swing was grooved, his putts were straight, and his short game was flawless. Without the double bogeys on the eighteenth and fourteenth holes he might have scored ninety five, and if hadn't taken three penalty stokes for being out-of-bounds, he could easily have shot ninety! Ninety! That was only one shot per hole more than the pros!

He savored every minute of the occasion, it was drinks all round in the club house and dinner on him for his golfing partners. He was careful to remember the clubs that he had used, the clothes that he had worn and the golf cart that he had driven in.

"I want that cart every time I play," he joked with the boys in the pro shop. "I'll even buy it from you."

Two weeks passed before he found the time to return to Florida to play again. He changed in the locker room into his now familiar golf clothes and proceeded to the starter's kiosk to meet the other members of the foursome. He recognized his buddies, but could not believe his eyes, when he saw that they were sitting in red golf carts.

"We have to change carts," he said.

"But why? These are new. They're great. They even have a GPS position for each hole."

"I have to have my green cart. I can't play in this one."

The starter overheard their conversation.

"They were sold," he said.

Tony scored a hundred and twelve. He hadn't played that badly for months. He knew it was the red cart. After his miserable game he sought out the club manager and demanded that he tell him where the green golf carts had gone. He was shown a copy of the check that the club had received as payment for the carts. He made a note of the name of the dealer who had purchased the carts. He had to buy his cart. It was imperative that he found it and not just because he was superstitious. A visit to the dealer's yard on the following Monday only added to his frustration when he was told that the carts had been shipped to the Bahamas. With a little friendly persuasion Tony was able to find the name of the company in Harbour Island that had purchased fourteen of the carts. All he could remember about 'his' cart was its number. It was twenty something, six or seven, he wasn't exactly sure, but he was sure that it was a number in the twenties. The dealer confirmed that those carts numbered sixteen through thirty had been shipped to Herman's in Harbour Island.

The next morning Tony flew to Nassau where he boarded the Bo Hengy, a fast catamaran-hulled ferry boat that makes daily trips to both Spanish Wells and Harbour Island. As the ferry boat approached the dock in Spanish Wells he looked down from his seat on the upper deck and counted eighteen golf carts. He saw rows and rows of them for rent from Abners or Gemini, some were red or blue, but most were green, just like the one he hoped to find in Harbour Island. He wondered if there would be fewer of them there. When the last of the passengers who were disembarking in Spanish Wells had made their way off the ferry and those who were traveling on to the next destination had boarded, Tony watched as the boat maneuvered its way around Gun Point and through the channel that is bordered by the Devil's Backbone. Thirty minutes later Dunmore Town came into view. Tony had never seen so many golf carts. They were everywhere and in all the colours of the rainbow. Two seaters, four seaters and even six seaters.

Buggies for rent signs were displayed on hand-held signs being held aloft for the newly arriving tourists to see, or displayed on the sides of the carts that jostled with each other in an attempt to find the most advantageous position. Tony scanned the crowd for Herman's sign. He spotted it at the back of the crowd being held up by a kid who was no older than ten or twelve. The kid looked tired and disinterested in his job; it was evident that he was there to fulfill some obligation to Herman. Tony pushed his way through the crowd of peddlers until he reached Herman's emissary.

The Kantaberry Tales

"I'd like to rent a buggy," he said to the kid.

"Jump in," the kid replied in amazement.

For a ten year old he was a fearless driver. Tony was thankful that the buggy only had a top speed of ten miles per hour; he could only imagine the mayhem that would have been caused if the vehicle had had a speed of thirty or forty. They drove a few blocks away from the dock area along a maze of poorly paved roads until the kid turned into a yard that was packed with green golf carts.

A heavy-set Brilander approached them.

"I'm Herman," he announced in a heavily accented voice that Tony had difficulty understanding. He told the delivery kid to get back to the dock and extended his hand. Tony was reluctant to shake this man's greasy hand, but against his better judgment, he did.

"You need a buggy?"

"Yes."

"We got plenty," he laughed out loud at his own humour.

Tony knew that he needed to be careful in dealing with this man. He didn't want to arouse any suspicions. He needed a specific buggy.

"I like green," Tony offered, "and my lucky number is twenty six".

"Right there," Herman indicated, "just came in a couple of weeks ago. Forty dollars a day. How many days do you want it?"

"Just overnight," he replied as he handed Herman forty dollars. "Do you want to see my driver's license?"

"Nah."

Tony drove out of Herman's yard, made a turn towards the beach on a deserted road he had seen when the kid had been driving earlier. He drove all the way to the end of the road and came to a stop under a large flowering tree. He looked around to make sure that no one was watching him, he grabbed the two plastic containers of sand from their holders behind the seat and dumped their contents on the ground. With his fingers he sifted through the sand looking for something. What ever it was, it wasn't there. Just sand.

"Damn," he said aloud.

Now he was in a quandary. How could he go back and change buggies without alerting Herman to the fact that he was looking for something. An idea came to him as he drove the buggy back to Herman's yard.

The Kantaberry Tales

"Hi," he called.

"Somethin' wrong?"

"It's my girlfriend. She refuses to ride in the buggy because of the number."

"You picked it. Don't sound too lucky to me," he laughed.

"You see, the two and the six can be divided into one another to give three, and three is an evil omen, she says. Any way she won't ride in it. Can I change it?"

"Sure," Herman agreed with some annoyance.

Tony picked number twenty five. He was sure that was the one.

He followed the same road as he had before in number twenty six. He parked in the same spot and emptied the two containers of sand onto the ground. Nothing except sand!

He couldn't go back again.

Tony drove to the Pink Sands Hotel, checked into a luxury room and went to the bar for a much needed drink. He'd decided that he would tackle the buggy problem the next day.

Maybe it was twenty four? He was almost sure that it was twenty something. But suppose it wasn't? Was he losing his mind? No, he remembered that on the day when he had broken a hundred, one of his buddies had remarked that his score was exactly four times the number on the golf cart and that in the future he should use a cart with a lower number if he wanted to shoot a lower score. It was definitely twenty five. He'd checked the correct buggy.

He ordered another drink. His face turned a shade whiter as he thought of the consequences that his failure to produce the key would bring. The key was to a locker that contained a fortune, a fortune that belonged to someone else, not him. His cut was only a small portion of the total amount, but large enough to sustain him for a number of years. He had hidden the key in the sand as a precaution on the day he'd scored a hundred. He'd been carrying the key in his pocket, it was heavy and cumbersome and it distracted him from his game. He had looked for a safe place to keep it, and decided that the sand container was perfect. After all he never took a divot so he had no use for the sand. He suspected that the constant jiggling of the cart had provided sufficient movement to make the heavy key sink into the sand and bury itself. Out of sight out of mind. He was so ecstatic about his score that he forgot all about the key until it was too late.

"You look as though you've lost your best friend," a female voice remarked.

"Worse," Tony commented without looking up.

"Tell me about it."

"It's a long story."

"I've got time."

Her name was Kris. She was a model. Tony ordered another drink for himself and one for Kris. She drank vodka and kantaberry juice. They had another. And another. He told her the story. She laughed when he had finished.

"I'm a dead man," he proclaimed.

"What's in the locker?" she asked.

"I don't know."

"And where is it?"

"I don't know that either."

"And who are you supposed to give the key to."

Tony shrugged his shoulders.

"It's complicated. We're all unconnected messengers. Like links in a chain. I don't have any idea who the other links are."

"Somebody must know."

"Sure, but I don't want to think about that."

"What are you going to do?" Kris asked.

"First I'm gonna have another drink, and then I'm gonna take you to dinner, and then? We'll see what happens."

He returned buggy number twenty five to Herman's the following morning.

"Everythin' all right?" Herman asked with his customary laugh.

Tony had decided that he would have to fabricate a plausible story that would somehow permit him to examine the sand containers on every one of the fourteen buggies that had arrived from Florida. It was possible that they had been moved from one buggy to another during their trip.

"What are these containers of sand for?" Tony asked innocently.

"Cigarette butts," replied Herman.

Tony was taken unawares. He had not expected that answer to his question.

"We encourage our customers to put their butts in the sand instead of littering the streets," Herman volunteered.

"Do all your buggies have them?"

"Just about," he answered.

"And how many buggies do you own?"

"Sixty-four," Herman answered proudly.

"So you routinely clean these containers out and replace them?"

"Every week, sometimes twice if we have some heavy smokers. Why you askin' all these questions?"

Tony explained that his girl friend had rented a cart some while ago and she thought that she might have lost her keys in the sand.

"Why would she put her keys in the sand? Don't make no sense."

"She had her hands full and needed something out of her pocket; she placed her keys on the nearest convenient place she could find, I guess. Did you find them?"

"No."

"When you clean the containers, do you empty them out?"

"No, my boy just collects them all together and picks out the butts".

"So the keys could still be hidden in the sand?"

"It's possible, I s'pose."

"I'd like to check."

"All of them?"

"Yes. I'll pay you a hundred dollars."

Tony spent the rest of the day emptying all the containers, sifting through the sand with his fingers and then refilling them. The missing locker key wasn't there.

Herman told him that there were twelve buggies out on rental, which meant that there were an additional twenty-four containers to check. He waited around for two more days for the buggies to be returned. Still nothing.

At dinner that evening, while they shared a bottle of 1968 kantaberry wine, he told Kris that he had exhausted all the possibilities and that his only choice was to return to Palm Beach to meet his doom.

It could have been the effect of the wine; a light went on in his befuddled brain. Maybe she was the next link in the chain? It was an unusual coincidence to have found such an attractive girl on her own in the hotel, and one who obviously had no plans.

When she suggested that she accompany him to Florida, he was sure that his instincts about her were correct.

Kris said goodbye to him at the Fort Lauderdale airport, saying as she left, "I'll see you around."

Tony returned to his normal life, but kept a wary eye open to see if he was being tailed. He was constantly looking over his shoulder. On Saturday he played golf at the Country Club with the other three members of his usual foursome. They noticed Tony's nervousness.

"Relax Tony. You're all wound up."

"I know, I'm sorry."

Tony hit slice after slice as he played the worst front nine of his golfing career. He told his buddies to play on without him.

"You guys go ahead. I'll stay here and have a few drinks," he suggested. He remained in the clubhouse for two hours where he consumed too many drinks. He was slumped over a table when his three friends came to join him. After a little coaxing he told them the story of the sand, the fruitless search of the buggies, and his anxiety over the loss of the locker key. He purposely omitted any mention of Kris.

It was his golfing partner who provided the solution. He had sat with Tony in cart number twenty five on the day that Tony had broken a hundred.

"I remember it as if it was yesterday," he began. "We were on the seventeenth fairway, I was keeping score and I knew that with a bogey bogey finish you could break a hundred. You hooked your drive into the rough; I drove you over to where your ball was lying, dropped you off with your seven iron, then went to play my ball, which was in the fairway, I might add! A golfer from another hole, the eighth I believe, had sliced his ball into our fairway. His ball was sitting close to mine. So, while I was waiting for the seventeenth green to clear, I told him to go ahead. He played a beautiful five iron shot over the trees onto the eighth green, just like a pro. He took a huge divot, something that none of us ever do, which he carefully replaced, and then he asked if he could use the sand from the container on our cart to fill in the hole that still remained. He poured a generous amount of sand into the hole, and as he did a key fell out. He asked me if it was mine, when I told him that it wasn't, he said that he'd leave it at the pro shop."

"You mean it's been here all the time?" Tony screamed as he rushed off to the pro shop.

"I guess so," his three buddies laughed after him.

He told the assistant pro, who was working behind the counter in the pro shop, that he had lost a locker key a few weeks ago and that he had just learned that it had been handed in. There was a box under the counter that contained sunglasses, lighters and an assortment of articles that had been left on the golf carts. The assistant pro rummaged around the bottom of the box and produced a locker key. The relief flooded through Tony.

"I'll take that."

It was Kris. She appeared from nowhere, took the key from the open-mouthed assistant pro, tucked the key into her pocket and disappeared as quickly as she had arrived.

LAUNDRY

Melanie Pinder sat in her law office above the Royal Bank and quietly surveyed her surroundings. She had come a long way from her humble beginnings and she was proud of herself and the sign on her door that read,

'Melanie Pinder. Attorney at Law'.

She was the first member of her family to attend college; in fact she was the first to complete high school. She had attended school in Nassau before passing her college entrance exams that awarded her a place at a college in London. She had chosen a career in law on the advice of her Father who had always said that what the Bahamas needed was more local lawyers. She'd completed her law degree then continued on with further studies in criminology.

Derek Hawkins

Her office had been open for eighteen months. The first five months had been slow as the local people had taken their time to warm up to her. She didn't fit their idea of what a lawyer should be. But slowly they came around as her expertise became known throughout the island, and now a steady stream of clients kept her hopping. Her practice consisted of mostly property transfers by both visitors and locals. Someone was always selling and someone was always buying and quite often there was a problem of title or a will that wasn't exactly clear. She had handled three divorces, a child custody case, two motor-cycle accident settlements and a dispute between a group of fishermen who claimed shares in one of the lobster fishing boats. It was a far cry from criminal law, but she derived a great deal of satisfaction from the work that she performed.

Her personal life had not fared as well as her business one. She had met a man on the plane when she had been returning home after completing her schooling in London. He was everything that she wasn't. He was twelve years older then she was, he was Caucasian, a petty thief, married with a daughter, a gambler and, as her mother had said when she had met him, 'he's touched by the devil'. But she had fallen head over heels in love with this man. He'd made her laugh, he'd made her cry, he'd made her feel special, he'd introduced her to a way of life that she thought could only happen to other people and above all else, he'd loved her. And now he was serving time in prison because of her. He had decided to 'go straight', to earn her trust so they could be married. They'd purchased a beautiful home on the beach where they had lived in domestic bliss for fourteen months. They'd already picked their wedding day and their honeymoon location, when he had been arrested and tried for bank robbery. He was now serving three years in prison in England. She wondered if he would come back after his release. It was difficult to talk intimately on the telephone, and each time that they did she had the same frightening thought that his feelings for her had changed. She understood his predicament, she realized that he felt cheated and she could also appreciate his reluctance to talk about their future while he was still incarcerated. Neither of them had any idea of the depth of their love for each other; if they had, they would have known that they were both capable of enduring the long wait until the time came when they would be together again. She missed David more than she would have thought that it was possible to miss anyone. He was her life. He had to come back.

Melanie had scheduled a meeting with a man named Ferguson. He had called her secretary a week ago to say that he would be visiting Spanish Wells for a day and hoped that she would be able to see him. He had given no indication as to what the meeting would entail. He arrived at her office at ten after his journey from Nassau on the Fast Ferry. He was man of about fifty with a red face that had obviously been exposed to the weather for most of its life. His hair was white and thick, his eyes were dark brown, almost black, and they never met Melanie's as she shook hands with him and offered him a seat.

"Andrew Ferguson," he stated as her took her hand and the seat. "You'll be wondering why I'm here?" he said with a grin.

"I'm curious."

"I want you to represent me in the purchase of a house on Harbour Island."

"Which one? I'm familiar with most of the homes that are for sale there."

"Shangri La. It's on four acres on the beach."

"I'm familiar with the property."

If only you knew, she thought. Shangri La had been owned by a friend of David's and it was where she and David had really gotten to know each other. It had been their first date together. The owner had subsequently been indicted for numerous crimes and had been forced to sell his estate. Melanie knew that the asking price was in the region of six million dollars.

"I'd like you to handle the paperwork for me. I'll be away for much of the time and I need someone to keep an eye on the place for me after I've bought it."

"I could arrange that for you."

"I'll wire money into your escrow account."

"Let's wait until after the closing," Melanie suggested. "Have you made an offer on the property yet?" she inquired.

"Not yet. I want you to do that for me. Pay them whatever they want."

"They're asking six million, I believe."

"That's my understanding. I'll wire you the money."

"All of it?" Melanie asked incredulously.

"Yes. Plus your fees and some for a caretaker. Seven million should be about right. If you'll give me your escrow account number, I'll wire the money from Nassau tomorrow."

Melanie handed Andrew Ferguson a card that included her wiring instructions and watched as he exited her office.

She sat back in her office chair and exhaled audibly. It was ironic that she would be involved in the sale of Shangri La. The place held wonderful memories for her and her eyes filled with tears as she thought of David and the wonderful day that they had spent together there. It now seemed so long ago. She folded her arms onto her desk in an attitude of momentary despair, then she lowered her head to her arms and cried.

"A penny for your thoughts."

Melanie couldn't believe it. It was David's voice. She leapt up from her chair expecting to see him standing there. He wasn't, but an attractive brunette was. The brunette whisked her dark wig from her head and stepped around her desk.

It was him!

Between a mixture of tears and passionate kisses the questions poured out. Slowly David told her why and how he happened to be there in her office dressed as a woman and not in prison.

They sat together on the floor in the corner of her office, he with his arms wrapped around her and she wedged between his legs with her arms around his neck. They kissed after each sentence.

"I'm working undercover for the Bahamian police."

"You never said anything."

"I was sworn to secrecy. I shouldn't be here now."

The Kantaberry Tales

"Are you in danger?"

"I don't think so."

"What are you doing then?"

"Tailing Mr. Ferguson."

"Why?"

"It's a long story. What was he doing here?"

"He's buying Charlie's estate, so he says. He said he would wire transfer seven million dollars to me from Nassau tomorrow."

"I'm sure he will. Make sure that you advise the authorities as soon as his money arrives. For your own protection."

"Is he a criminal?"

"We think he's skimming money from a casino. I'm just watching him and reporting what I find to the police."

"But why you?"

"Ferguson is the Purser on a cruise ship. He looks after all the money on his ship, he pays the bills when the ship is docked in Nassau and he deposits the proceeds from the casino in the ship's bank account. The ship's owners have suspected for some time that large sums of money were being skimmed. They went to the Bahamian police, who consulted with Scotland

Yard and my old friend Ted Newman, he's a Chief Inspector now, paid me a visit in prison to enlist my help."

"Your help?"

"Yes, as strange as it may sound. Ted and I used to play in a band together many years ago and we have remained friends. I've worked for him before, you know; once, I remember he needed a safe opened, and another time he asked if I could identify another safe cracker's identity by the method he used. This time he needed me to play the role of a lounge entertainer onboard a cruise ship. He knew that I was still a pretty good piano player and singer. I agreed to do the job on one condition."

"Which was?"

"That when the job was finished, I would be released from prison and allowed to return to the Bahamas. The Bahamian authorities agreed, and as they say in England, 'Bob's yer uncle.'"

"How long have you been out of prison?"

"Three weeks today."

"And why the disguise? Do you wear it all the time?"

"This is the first and last time. I followed him here on the Ferry. He would have spotted me without it; it's not a very large vessel."

"Except for the voice, you would've fooled me."

"I fooled your secretary. She had no idea".

"How much time do we have?"

"I have to go back on the Ferry this afternoon. I'm expected to play in the lounge this evening."

They had three hours together that afternoon. Melanie drove her 'girl friend' home for lunch. They never had time for lunch. Watching him struggle to get his bra off without ripping it put Melanie into a fit of hysterical convulsive laughter and, when he stepped out of the dress with a move that would put any stripper to shame; she thought she would die laughing.

"Keep the pearls on," she managed to scream between her belly laughs, "they really turn me on."

If either of them had had any doubts about their future together, those doubts were dispelled that afternoon. They made love with a passion that took their respective breaths away. Locked in an embrace and bonded as close as Siamese twins they conversed with their bodies with an understanding that is reserved for lovers. Theirs was a desire that had grown more intense as the months had gone by, and now they released all of their emotions in a culmination of fervor and tenderness. From the very first time they met their love making had always been intense, but on this afternoon it reached a level of intensity that neither of them ever thought possible.

"I love you so much," David whispered. "I thought about this reunion all the time I was away."

"I thought that you might not come back," she confessed. "I don't know what I would have done if you hadn't."

It was only after David reassured her that if all went according to plan she could expect him to be back in less than a month as a free man, that she finally allowed him to don his disguise and return to the Ferry. David found a window seat on the port side of the Ferry where he could feign sleep and avoid any contact with his fellow passengers. The last thing he needed was to be picked up by a horny Bahamian. He watched as Ferguson boarded at the last minute and immediately proceeded to the upper deck for a smoke. The one and a half hour trip to Nassau was uneventful, and after changing clothes in the taxi that conveyed him back to the ship, much to the taxi driver's amusement, David breathed a long sigh of relief. By nine o'clock he was seated at the piano ready for another evening's performance.

Chief Inspector Edward Newman had visited the North Sea Camp Prison, where David was a guest of Her Majesty's Government a little over a month ago. When David had been ordered to the Warden's office, he had immediately thought that he would be reprimanded. He had been shocked to find his old friend Ted waiting for him. The Inspector had explained the assignment in detail, emphasizing the need for caution and repeating over and over again that David's function was to be that of an observer.

"I don't want any heroics," he stated, "just watch and report back. You understand?"

"My days of being a hero are over."

The terms of his employment had been ratified; he was officially released into Ted's custody, taken to London and briefed. He had been given a new identity, a glowing resume that would pass the scrutiny of any employer, a complete wardrobe of fashionable clothes, two valid credit cards and a wad of cash. He had been supplied with the name and number of a Bahamian Police official that he was to use only in an extreme emergency, and he was shown a dossier on Ferguson. He auditioned for the position of piano-bar entertainer and got the job easily. He boarded 'Dreamchaser' in Miami a week later.

David was an instant success. The piano bar, which had rarely attracted more than a handful of late night drunks, became one of the most popular places on the ship. He began at nine o'clock and played until two in the morning and every night the line of patrons waiting for a seat began forming as early as seven. He held his audience in the palm of his hand as he played their requests and astounded them with his pianistic skills. He played everything from jazz to classics, from Nat King Cole to Billy Joel; he even donned a pair of oversize sunglasses and sang a medley of Elton John favorites almost as well as the man himself.

He usually slept until eleven in the morning in the private cabin that had been assigned to him. He was popular with his fellow crew members, they were drawn to him like flies, and he was propositioned by both female crew members and passengers on a regular basis, so much so that he rarely had any privacy. But he kept his nose clean. His thoughts were always centered on Melanie.

He bumped into Ferguson in the men's room during a break one evening. David saw his reflection in the mirror as he was washing his hands.

"I like the way you play," he said.

"Thanks."

The Kantaberry Tales

"The piano bar is making good money now."

"I'm glad."

"Are you being treated OK?"

"Fine. Thanks."

"Keep up the good work."

David excused himself and went back to work.

The 'Dreamchaser' cruised between Miami and Nassau on a regular schedule; a three day trip followed by a four day trip, week in and week out throughout the year. Her capacity was sixteen hundred passengers and she ran close to ninety percent of capacity. They lounged in the sun during the day, ate four meals a day, drank at the numerous bars, partied into the night and gambled in the casino. It was rumored that the money that the ship made in the casino was more than enough to cover the cost of the complete operation. She was owned by a British company and registered in the Bahamas. The shortages in the casino receipts had been reported to the Bahamian officials who, because of the registration of the vessel, would be required to conduct an investigation and would have jurisdiction in any case that might result. They in turn had sought the assistance of Scotland Yard. Any theft of the magnitude of the one that the owners of the ship suspected was taking place would have a detrimental effect on all the ships that visited the Bahamas on a regular basis. The cruise ship business was of vital importance to the Bahamas and the order to apprehend the thieves had come from the highest level of the Government.

David had been smart enough to appreciate the importance of his role in this investigation and he had made his residency status in the country a condition of his acceptance. Under normal conditions, as a convicted felon, it would have been extremely doubtful that he would be allowed to reside in the Bahamas, and thus his life with Melanie would have been in jeopardy.

During its stay in Nassau the ship was moored at the St. George's Dock. It was here that Ferguson, as the Purser, was at his busiest. He contracted and paid for all the services that were performed by the local vendors. He also deposited the cash from the casino and all the fares from the passengers in the bank. The tax free status within the Bahamas which extended to ships of Bahamian registration was of crucial importance to the balance sheet of the ship's operations. There were detailed formulae that had been established over many years that could project to within a few dollars the net spending capabilities of the passengers, and a continuing shortfall in this projected amount had been the first signal that someone was skimming the take. Based on their demographics and the number of passengers on each trip it was clear that the casino returns had fallen by five percentage points over the past two years. This amount translated into many millions of dollars. As the Purser, Ferguson had become the prime suspect, but the police needed evidence. He needed to be caught in the act, or if he was part of a sophisticated money laundering cartel, they needed to keep him and his contacts under strict surveillance until they made a mistake.

'Just observe. Don't be a hero' were the words that David repeated to himself as he nervously followed Ferguson ashore. He walked along Bay Street, keeping Ferguson in sight. He waited across the street for him to exit Barclay's Bank. His first stop. He watched as he entered The Royal Bank, his second stop, and then the Fidelity Bank, his third stop. It was reasonable to assume that the ship's business was conducted with several banks, David thought.

Ferguson's next stop, number four, was at the law offices of Smith and Johnson. David waited in a café, across the street from the office, where he sat in the window and nursed a cup of coffee. He noted the time and the length of the visit in a note book. Next stop, number five, was at the office of Knowles, Higgs and Bethel. He stayed for almost an hour. He made a sixth stop at another lawyer's office and then he returned to the ship. It all seemed innocent enough.

David reported Ferguson's movements to Ted as he had been instructed.

Four days later, on the next visit to Nassau by the ship, Ferguson visited the same three banks but two different attorneys. David filed his report.

Ferguson enjoyed listening to David play and he become a regular visitor to the piano bar, where he usually sat at a table close to the raised dais where the piano was located, or if he was early enough, he would sit at one of the seats that surrounded the piano. He liked to join in the choruses of the songs that he knew and his rich baritone voice could often be heard reverberating around the room. He sang loudly, especially if he was a little inebriated.

The usually secretive Mr. Ferguson, who was well under the influence, confided in David.

"I'm off on a trip tomorrow," he whispered.

"To where?" David asked as he turned his head away from his microphone.

"Spanish Wells!"

David's heart skipped a beat and his fingers lost their magic for a moment, as he asked cautiously, "Where's that?"

"Not far, just a boat ride away. I leave at seven, so I'm off to bed. Good night."

Why was he going to Spanish Wells? What business could he have there? It was too late to contact the Inspector for instructions and this wasn't a dire emergency that warranted a call to the Bahamian Police.

"I can't observe if he's in Spanish Wells and I'm here," David rationalized. "I have to go with him."

On the pretense that he would be paying tribute to Cher during his performance the following evening, he borrowed a black wig and a selection of women's clothes from the cruise director. Back in his cabin he tried on the clothes and made a few adjustments to make them comfortable. He couldn't believe that he was actually doing this. He packed his 'purse' with a few essentials and bright and early the next morning he followed Ferguson to the Fast Ferry terminal on Potter's Cay, where they both boarded the vessel for the trip to Spanish Wells. His excitement made him want to pee and he almost blew his cover as he turned the handle to the men's room before realizing that he would have to use the ladies. He knew that he was supposed to keep his identity a secret, but there was no way he could return to Spanish Wells and not see Melanie. She would be so surprised.

But it was David who had been surprised as he had watched Ferguson climb the stairs up to Melanie's office.

David telephoned a few days later and, after telling her how much he missed her, he asked her if the wire transfer from Ferguson had been executed.

"Seven million," she said "just like the man said."

"Any instructions?"

"No, he said he would be in touch."

"You could write yourself a check and take off."

"I'm thinking about it," she laughed.

"And you informed the authorities?"

"Yes. I sent a copy of the transfer to the Central Bank."

"That's good. I'll call when I'm back in Nassau to see if he's been in touch with you. Hang on to the money. I love you."

David filed his report to the Inspector later that day, giving an accurate account of all that had taken place.

He was surprised to receive a phone call from England in such quick response to his report.

"Do you know this lawyer?"

"Yes."

"Can she be trusted do you think?"

"I'm sure she can. She's my fiancée; we're getting married as soon as this caper is over."

"So, she's the one."

When 'Dreamchaser' returned to Miami, David was greeted by a plain clothes cop from England. He escorted him to the airport where David boarded a flight to London. In the Chief Inspector's office he was handed a manila file that contained his passport, his driver's license and an official document that confirmed his release from prison. Much to his surprise there was another document that expunged his record from the files, thus providing him with an untarnished reputation.

"I wasn't expecting this."

"It was the least we could do. You did a good job for us. We'll take it from here."

"I'm fired?"

"You're free to go."

"But what about Ferguson?"

"Just leave him to us. If your fiancée receives any instructions from him, which I doubt she will, tell her to obey them and then inform the Bahamian police."

Ted extended his hand to David and wished him bon voyage "Keep your nose clean and have a nice life."

David flew to Nassau that evening and then caught the Ferry to Spanish Wells the following morning. He'd called Melanie from Nassau when he'd landed. His home-coming was celebrated in private for three days. They only came out of their house to buy food; the rest of the time was spent on the beach, in the garden or in bed. They made up for a lot of lost time.

Melanie received another wire transfer from Ferguson, this one in the amount of two and a half million dollars.

She sent a copy of the wire to the Central Bank.

They were married six weeks later in a small family ceremony in Harbour Island, where they also enjoyed a relaxing honeymoon at Runaway Hill. One morning at breakfast David noticed a report in the newspaper that mentioned the cruise ship. It stated that the Company had been forced to sell 'Dreamchaser' to a

Greek shipping company and that she was now cruising the Greek islands.

Little by little they were able to piece together the whole story.

A warrant had been issued for the arrest of Andrew Ferguson but he was never apprehended. He mysteriously disappeared; it was suggested that he was disposed of by his colleagues. A minority owner of the cruise ship had devised an infallible scheme to launder the proceeds of his drug business through the casino. In essence the plan was simple. Large amounts of illegal cash were distributed to dozens of gamblers who gambled in the casino on board the ship. These gamblers purposely lost their money by placing large foolish bets. The money from the casino was then deposited in the ship's accounts in Nassau. Ferguson had realized that something fishy was going on, so each time he made a deposit for the ship he made a deposit in his own account. He started small but then became greedy. The police reported that he stole almost sixty million dollars from the ship's accounts. As instructed by his bosses, he selected a number of prominent law companies throughout the Bahamas and, under the guise of a potential land purchaser he transferred huge amounts of cash into their escrow accounts. The land transactions never materialized and the money was eventually withdrawn from the escrow accounts to other offshore banks, from which it was routed back to Columbia. The Bahamian authorities investigated the involvement of these law companies and several of them were closed for failure to comply with the trust laws.

Several months passed by, the summer weather threatened time after time but David and Melanie were fortunate enough to escape any violent storms. The stress-free life agreed with David, he became an avid fly fisherman and could often be seen wading through the shallow waters at the western end of Spanish Wells. He rarely caught any fish, but he didn't mind. Never a day went by that he didn't thank God for his good fortune in finding this place and his beautiful bride.

Melanie also felt blessed. Married life agreed with her and she found pleasure in cooking David's favorite foods, and with her mother's help she produced several jars of kantaberry jelly from the fruit of the bushes that grew in profusion in their yard. She was also a successful attorney, well respected and well liked. She devoted a portion of her time to those who needed legal advice but couldn't afford it and she felt fulfilled. She had a loving husband who made even the most routine event seem special and she too gave thanks to God for sending him to her.

They also gave thanks to Andrew Ferguson. His nine and a half million was still on deposit in the escrow account earning four percent interest.

"As my old Mum used to say, it's better than a poke in the eye with a blunt stick," commented David every morning.

THE CURE

Chuck Holstrem had a passion for fly-fishing. He subscribed to two weekly publications that featured articles on the equipment used successfully by fellow advocates of the sport. He studied the magazines and read them from cover to cover, sometimes in the bathroom but usually in his office at work when he thought that nobody was looking. At home he tied his own flies, basing his designs on those that he had heard were used by the experts. He kept them all in carefully labeled plastic containers that he fitted neatly into his tackle box. He purchased the correct clothes from a fishing catalogue; he wanted to look as though he knew what he was doing. He bought his rods and reels based on the recommendations of the magazine editor. He had it all, a hat with a band to hold his flies, a sleeveless jacket with a zillion pockets to hold all the paraphernalia that the expert fly-fisherman required and waders that would allow him to venture into deep water if his catch happened to take off. A wicker basket to hold whatever he was lucky enough to catch completed his getup. He actually used the basket to hold a sandwich and a coke.

He fished in the streams and rivers of his home province of Ontario, where the water was cold but clear and the trout that he was hoping to catch were virtually non-existent. Chuck was a born optimist and every weekend he would load his Jeep wagon and head for a more remote location where he had been told that the fish were as thick as flies. If they were, he must have picked an off day, because his wicker basket was always empty when he returned home. He'd consumed the sandwich and the coke. He did catch a couple of sun fish one day and on another occasion he hooked a catfish, but they didn't count.

After a visit to the Sportsman Show held at the Toronto Exhibition grounds, he signed up for casting classes to improve his ability in showing the fish the fly more quickly and more accurately. While he was at the show he collected a number of free brochures which he jammed into a plastic bag. The bag had a picture of a trout leaping for a fly printed on its side. He used the bag to carry his lunch to work each day, until the bag disintegrated from too much use. Before it fell apart, the bag did however attract the attention of Joanne Simpson. She worked in the same building as Chuck, but on a different floor. All the occupants of the building used the same parking lot. Coincidentally her truck happened to be parked next to his Jeep. She saw him carrying the bag. She made a comment about the attractiveness of the trout and said something about wishing that she could catch one just like it. Chuck had never known a girl with an interest in fishing; he had always assumed that it was a sport reserved exclusively for men. He waited for her in the parking lot after work and invited her for a drink.

He drove her to a bar that he had heard about but had never been to, that was owned by an avid fisherman with a reputation of being able to catch the elusive 'big ones'. The interior of the bar was decorated in the style of a fishing lodge with mounted fish adorning the walls and hundreds of pictures of the owner and his friends displaying their many near-limit catches. The owner and his wife greeted Joanne like a long lost friend when she entered with Chuck.

"You've been here before?" Chuck asked. It was as much a question as a statement of fact.

"It's my favorite watering hole," she acknowledged.

They sat at a small rustic table with fishing flies embedded under forty coats of varnish on its surface and talked about fishing.

It was all too much for Chuck to handle at one time. She actually seemed to enjoy his company and his conversation. She showed no sign of being bored by his fishing stories, unlike every other girl he had ever dated, and she even shared several of her own. She drank beer like one of the guys, she rolled her own cigarettes, she swore like a proverbial sailor and her clothes reminded Chuck of the girl on the cover of the L.L. Bean catalog.

Their evening together flew by and when she shook hands with him outside of the trailer where she lived, her grip was something to behold. They made a date to go fishing together the following Saturday.

Joanne drove. As she explained, she knew this great spot and her truck had four-wheel drive in case they got stuck. Chuck liked the way that she drove with her elbow halfway out of the driver's side window, the country music radio station on loud and her cigarette dangling from her lips. She had the pack tucked inside the sleeve of her rolled up T-shirt. She sang along with the music in a voice reminiscent of Dolly Parton on one of her worse days. She knew most of the words to the songs, but if she didn't or couldn't recall them fast enough, she la-di-dahed for a few bars, banged loudly on the outside of the truck door with her sun-burned arm, and yelled some obscenity that she thought was highly amusing because she laughed like a drain and repeated the process over again.

She drove northwest to Brampton, then north for thirty miles into the hills to the head-waters of the Humber River. She left the paved road and followed a dirt path which eventually petered out and became nothing more than two ruts through the trees and rocks. She veered to the right and parked within six inches of an escarpment that overlooked a fast flowing shallow stream.

"This is it!" she announced. "Let's fish!"

Chuck had to get out on her side because she had parked so close to the edge. He was really pleased to see that Joanne had almost the identical equipment to his, same rod and reel, same waders, same hat and the same wicker basket.

"You fish here," she told him, "I'll go upstream a bit."

Chuck had always been of the opinion that complete silence was an essential requisite of fly-fishing, that any noise would spook the fish. He went to great lengths to make sure that he placed his feet carefully on the river bed so as to avoid making any undue noise or splash. He was dumbfounded to hear Joanne screaming uncomplimentary comments at the branches of the over-hanging trees that caught her line, or the slippery rocks that caused her to stumble. When she hooked the first fish, she berated it in language that would cause a trooper to blush. She repeated her barrage of foul language on the second, third, fourth and fifth fish that she landed. Chuck hadn't had a nibble.

"Try this," she told him as she tied one of her flies to his line. She tugged on his line and made a face. "Your line's too heavy."

She watched as he made a cast.

"Make a wider arc," she instructed. "Let the fly settle. Keep the tip up. There, by those rocks!"

Whether or not it was Joanne's perseverance with him or it was just a matter of time, Chuck finally landed his first brown trout. It was small but to Chuck it would always be his biggest prize. He placed it carefully in his wicker basket. What a day!

The next few weeks were the most exciting of Chuck's life as he and Joanne spent more and more time together. They fished every weekend and under Joanne's tutelage, Chuck gradually became an accomplished fly-fisherman.

Spending so much of their time together naturally led to a change in their relationship. The firm handshake had first been replaced by a peck on the cheek and just last night Joanne had taken his hand and placed it on her breast while she rammed her tongue into his mouth. He hadn't felt much because she still had her flannel shirt on over her T-shirt, but the message had been received loud and clear. He was expected to take it to the next level. He had to 'fish or cut bait'.

Chuck was attracted to Joanne, she was all any man could want, but he was petrified of becoming involved in a sexual relationship. He'd been with girls before, so that part wasn't the problem. His problem was a rash! A nasty rash that had developed over the past few weeks between his legs. His groin and the area around his crotch was inflamed, sore and a fiery red colour. He had purchased several anti-itch creams from the drug store, but none of them appeared to have any effect on the rash; it was getting worse. He knew that he would have to see a doctor soon, but he was embarrassed and a part of him was concerned that the rash might be a sign of the beginning of some more serious ailment. Syphilis, gonorrhea, hepatitis and AIDS were words that sprang to mind. Chuck was scared.

He made an appointment with Dr. Miroshani Patel, a dermatologist that had been recommended by the pharmacist that had sold him every brand of skin ointment that the drug store stocked. He sat nervously in the Doctor's waiting room reading a magazine. He read an advertisement for a bone-fishing camp in the Bahamas and surreptitiously tore it out and secreted it in his pocket. He twisted and turned on his seat as he tried to find a comfortable position; he wanted to scratch the rash but he couldn't without being noticed by the other patients waiting with him in the office.

Finally his name was called. A nurse led him to a small cubicle and told him to remove his clothes. Standing naked in the little room was heaven; he could scratch without being seen. He had already convinced himself that the Doctor must see hundreds of such cases a year, many of which were probably far worse than his, and having another man exam his most private parts would be just a routine.

The Doctor pushed open the door and entered. It was a girl, younger than him, with dark brown eyes, long black hair held back with a red barrette, and carrying a clip-board. He immediately dropped his hands to cover his affected area. She told him to lie down face up on the black vinyl-covered bench that had been covered with a white paper sheet.

"What seems to be the problem?" she asked as she walked around his prostrate body, surveying him like a mortician.

"I've got a rash," he replied meekly, "down there."

She lowered her head and peered at his crotch; she found a wooden tongue depressor and carefully lifted his penis to one side with it, while she examined his testicles.

"Does it itch?" she asked.

"All the time."

"And how long have you had it."

"I was born with it," Chuck replied.

"I meant the rash, not your penis," she said.

"Oh. About six weeks."

"We'll do a blood test and I'll prescribe a cream to alleviate the itching."

"Is it serious?"

"It doesn't appear to be. The blood test will tell."

He didn't tell Joanne about his Doctor's visit, but he did show her the bone-fishing advert that he'd torn from the magazine. It was partially out of guilt over not being ready to have intercourse with her that he asked her to join him on a bone-fishing excursion to the Bahamas. It really never occurred to him that such an invitation would necessitate their staying together and most likely sharing a bed. They rented a cottage on the beach in Spanish Wells where they were assured by the travel agent, who had rented the same cottage to other bone-fishermen, that the bonefish were right at their back door. They packed their entire fly-fishing gear into two back packs and with little more than the clothes on their respective backs, they boarded an Air Canada flight for Nassau. Chuck's blood test had proven to be negative, which was some consolation, but the rash was still painful and as ugly-looking as ever. He speculated that with a change in the weather the rash might clear up, but he was wrong. It became progressively worse.

On their third night in the beach-front cottage Chuck explained his problem to Joanne.

"It's not contagious," he told her "I've been tested."

He agreed to make love to her with the lights out.

"It's embarrassing," he said. "I don't want you to see it."

Joanne couldn't have cared less, but when Chuck had to stop prematurely, long before she had gotten into a rhythm, because of the pain caused by the abrasion from her prickly pubic hair, she became infuriated and stormed out of the cottage.

The next morning she dragged Chuck to the Clinic, but it was closed. She called the local doctor's office only to be told by his answering machine, that he was out of town. A check on the inventory of creams at the pharmacy yielded nothing different from those which Chuck had carried with him. Joanne was venting her frustration to all and sundry about the lack of adequate medical care, when she was overheard by Clarence Underwood.

"You sick?" he asked.

"Not exactly," Joanne responded. "My boyfriend's got a nasty rash."

"Let me see," he said to Chuck.

"It's between my legs," he explained.

"Is it sore and itchy?"

"Oh yes."

"Is the skin broken from all the scratching?"

"Oh yes."

"Then you need to see Miss Emily. She'll fix you right up."

"She will?"

"Sure. She's better than any doctor. Miss Emily can fix just about anything."

"Where can I find her?" Chuck asked desperately.

"She lives in Lower Bogue; I'd have to take you."

Miss Emily had practiced 'medicine' for as long as anyone of her neighbors could remember. She administered Life leaf or Ploppers to those who suffered from asthma or shortage of breath, and a variety of teas made from Kalanchoe, Hurricane weed, Kantaberry or Gamalamee to treat everything from simple colds and flu, to headaches, ulcers, stomach upsets and diarrhea. She had learned her trade from her Grandmother and she would pass on her secrets to her daughter. She always took her daughter with her when she went to collect the leaves from the many different plants she used in the preparation of her cures. They collected the pale yellow bark from the Sandalwood tree, the rich green leaves of the Nigly Whitey, the red shaggy bark from the Gumbolimbo and the blue berries from the Kantaberry bushes. She showed her daughter how to mash the leaves of the plants into a pulp using a hard round stone ball; sometimes she soaked the leaves and 'fried' them in a pan before crushing them into a pulp. These pulps were then incorporated into bitter tasting teas, poultices, powders and balms. Miss Emily rarely administered to white people, they had their own doctors to take care of them and most of them failed to understand the importance of the harmony that is required within the human body. She maintained that the introduction of unnatural substances into the body could often do more harm than good.

Clarence Underwood brought Chuck to see Miss Emily.

He had explained to Chuck and to Joanne that they were not to expect too much.

"She can be a cantankerous old woman sometimes. But she's good at what she does. The folks in these parts believe in her a hundred percent. Her powers are legendary."

"How much will she charge?" asked Chuck.

He was concerned about the cost of the visit, the cost of getting to Lower Bogue and he also wondered what Clarence's interest was in all this.

As if by telepathy Clarence explained his role.

"I'm a fishin' guide," he told them. "I've seen you fishin' off the beach. Ain't nothing there. I'll show you where the bone-fish are. Just hire me for a day."

They were both relieved to find that Clarence was a fisherman like them. They had an implicit trust in fellow anglers and they immediately felt much more comfortable in this stranger's company. They realized that he was just being helpful. They traveled by ferry to Jean's Bay, where they took a taxi to Lower Bogue. Just having Clarence along guaranteed that they would not be overcharged; at least that was what they both thought.

Miss Emily looked into Chuck's eyes with a penetrating stare that made him feel as though he was undergoing a psychological examination, she put one of her bony hands on his temple and winced. She looked at his posture and then she ran her hands over his body. She never uttered a word as she continued her evaluation.

Then she turned to Joanne.

"There's nothing wrong with me," she said defensively, "he's the one with the rash."

Miss Emily spooned a small quantity of a white powder into an envelope.

"Mix this with some hot milk until it makes a paste, add more milk and a teaspoon of lime juice and drink it before you go to bed."

Chuck accepted the envelope in silence.

Miss Emily wasn't finished. She took another white powder from her collection and spooned a small amount into another envelope.

"This is Picao Preto. Mix this with any kind of lotion and apply it to the rash. Drink plenty of kantaberry juice and come back in two days if it hasn't healed."

She was finished with her ministrations.

"Thank you very much," said Chuck. "How much do I owe you?"

"Five dollars if it doesn't work," she replied, "and a hundred if it does."

They both thought that she was joking. But she wasn't.

There was a small crowd of curious onlookers gathered outside of Miss Emily's house as word of the stranger's presence had quickly circulated through the town. Chuck felt very self-conscious as they walked the few steps to the waiting taxi.

Later that night, in the privacy of the cottage, Chuck applied the potion to his rash. He mixed the white powder with Nivea cream and spread the resulting paste over his affected groin. He also drank the mixture of milk, lime juice and the other powder before he went to sleep. If Miss Emily was a faith healer, then her magical cure was bound to work because Chuck had complete faith in her.

"How do you feel?" Joanne asked in the morning.

"I feel wonderful, ready for some serious fishing."

"And the rash?"

"No change," he replied disappointedly.

Today was to be their last day of fishing from the beach outside of the cottage. They had hired Clarence as their guide for the following day, and the day after that they would be heading home.

They fished on the flood tide and on the ebb, they fished in the shallowest water and the deepest, they fished in the early morning and late into the evening, they must have walked miles from the western end of the beach to the flats at the eastern end. They both wore the full gear of the true fly-fisherman, hat, waders, sleeveless jacket and wicker basket. Even though the water was warm and the sun was blistering hot, they were never tempted to remove any of their clothing. Apart for the annoying itch between his legs, Chuck was a happy camper. His relationship with Joanne had developed into one of friendship and trust. He had discovered a different side to her, a side that she hid behind her red-neck exterior. She wanted the same things as he did, a friend, a companion, someone to trust and to confide in, and someone who cared about you. When the rash was gone he knew that their sexual relations would reach new heights and he was anticipating a night of pure delight in the very near future.

The sun was sinking towards the horizon, casting a golden glow across the shallow water between the beach and Pierre Rocks when they decided to call it a day. They were both tired from a long day in the sun but were exhilarated by the shear beauty of their surroundings and the peacefulness of this deserted beach. This had been their first visit to the Bahamas and to Spanish Wells, and it had exceeded their wildest dreams. The people had been the most welcome surprise. It was Joanne who had first made the comparison.

"They're a lot like us," she had observed on their first day on the island. "They all drive pick ups, smoke like hillbillies and listen to that good ole country music!"

"They talk loud, too, and that accent reminds me of the folk from Nova Scotia."

"But really friendly," added Joanne.

"Good God-fearing people," Chuck commented.

Chuck was eager to inspect his rash. As soon as they were back inside the cottage he removed his waders, his trousers and his shorts and stood in front of the long mirror. It didn't look any better to him.

Joanne came to take a look and to give her assessment of Miss Emily's worth.

"Its worse," she stated off handedly. "You should get your money back."

"She did say two days."

"Two days, two weeks. She's an old phony!"

"I'll go back tomorrow, like she said, after we've been fishing with Clarence."

They spent another unsatisfying night together.

The next morning they caught the ferry to Jean's Bay where they were to meet Clarence. He had borrowed an old truck from one of his friends and was waiting patiently on the dock when the ferry arrived. Chuck and Joanne loaded their gear into the back of the truck, squeezed into the cab with Clarence and told him that they were looking forward to a great day of fishing.

"How's the rash?" he asked Chuck.

"About the same," he answered.

"Its worse," Joanne repeated her claim.

"I have to go back to see Miss Emily today."

"We'll drop by when we're finished fishing. About four."

The truck came to a halt at the water's edge where a flats boat was tied to an old rickety dock. They unloaded their gear from the back of the truck and at Clarence's suggestion they donned their fishing attire before taking their places in the boat. Clarence carried a bucket and a cooler from the truck and placed them in the boat as well.

The bight of Eleuthera is shallow. The sand bars at low tide are impassable to all but the knowledgeable. They stretch for miles and miles and as the tide ebbs shallow areas of water remain that become the feeding grounds for bonefish. Clarence had been born in Bogue and he knew every shallow pass through the sand bars. The sun was dazzling as it reflected off the shallow water but Clarence, who never wore sun glasses, saw every tell-tale fin of the bonefish from a distance of a hundred feet. Joanne and Chuck stood back-to-back in the bow scanning the water for the fish. Clarence had turned off the motor and was using a long pole to propel the boat forward. As he saw the fins of the fish he would say quietly, 'eleven o'clock' or 'two o'clock' to indicate their position in relation to the two fishermen. Chuck and Joanne would cast their flies in the direction that Clarence had told them, and time and again they were rewarded with a strike. By noon they had caught eight fish. It was the most exciting morning of fishing that either one of them had ever experienced. Clarence showed them how to play the fish and how to turn them; it often took thirty minutes to bring the fish to the boat and the landing net.

They paused for lunch and then both Joanne and Chuck fished for a while from the water instead of the boat. This gave them more room to cast and to spot the fish without the aid of Clarence. Chuck caught the biggest fish of the day after a thirty minute battle. Clarence estimated that it weighed close to four pounds. He opened the cooler and produced three bottles of Kalik.

"To the champion," he toasted.

It was the first beer that they had tasted since their arrival in Spanish Wells. They polished it off in a heart beat and opened two more.

"This is the life," yelled Chuck.

The beer had a dramatic effect on Joanne. She started swearing and cursing at the water, the fish, the sun and her companions. She chained-smoked her cigarettes and spat repeatedly into the water. It was the old Joanne reincarnated.

"We'd better get goin' to Miss Emily's," said Clarence.

They went by boat instead of returning to the truck and driving the truck to Lower Bogue. Joanne decided to remain in the boat rather than get into a fight with Miss Emily over her incompetence. She laid back and watched Clarence and Chuck walk the short distance to Miss Emily's old shack.

"You walk like a duck," she yelled after Chuck, as she noticed for the first time the way he waddled along.

Miss Emily was also watching the two men approach from her seat on the porch. Chuck waved to her when he saw her but she didn't respond. Now he could feel those eyes focused on him as he walked, like two penetrating lasers. He knew that the old crone was diagnosing his gait.

She never even asked about his rash.

"Lie there," she ordered. She pointed to an old bench by the porch. Chuck hesitated for a moment then complied.

"What have I got to lose", he conjectured.

"You got a sharp knife?" she asked Clarence.

Clarence had a very sharp fillet knife, which he handed to Miss Emily.

"Hold him still," she ordered.

Chuck felt his arms being gripped by Clarence. He wondered what on earth she was going to do. Panic struck him as she placed the sharp knife close to his crotch.

Derek Hawkins

"She's gonna castrate me," he thought.

But she didn't. She sliced two inches off the top of his rubber waders.

"Them's the problem," she stated. "They've bin chaffin'. You'll be better now. You owe me a hundred dollars."

Two days after they returned home the rash disappeared. Chuck convinced Joanne that drinking beer was not for her; she switched to white wine and Chuck proposed.

SHIPWRECK

Hector Fernandez arrived in the Bahamas one hundred and eight years after his great grandparents had been shipwrecked on the Devil's Backbone. He came with a single purpose in mind, to dive on the wreck of the Cienfuegos, the ship on which his great grandparents had traveled back in 1895, the year of the disaster. He came to the Valentine's Dive Center with no expectations of making any undersea discoveries, or of finding any part of the ship that had not been found long before. He just wanted to see first hand where the tragedy had taken place, where his ancestors had spent the worst few weeks of their lives and to visit the town of Spanish Wells, the community from which the rescue team had originated. It was important for Hector to find and meet with the descendents of those brave men and women who had risked their own lives to save the lives of others. He wondered how many of them knew, or even cared about the number of lives that had been shaped over the years from the survivors they had rescued. Hector understood that it was his great grandfather's vision that had ensured a life of prosperity for all the members of his family, and he owed a huge debt of gratitude to the local people, for without their help his great grandparents would have perished in the shipwreck. He could not imagine how his life might have unfolded without the security that he had inherited.

His great grandfather had invested his time and money in the manufacture of cigars, and now after more than a century later, Hector was the President of the enterprise. He had been given control of the family business after his own father had decided to flee from Cuba to Miami in the spring of 1978 and now he was in the Bahamas to capture the memory of his ancestors.

The dive boat departed from the dock at a few minutes after seven in the morning with a group of divers that included Hector, a couple from New Jersey, two girls from Jacksonville and two dive masters. The sea was flat and the diesel powered boat traveled at a high speed as they left Dunmore Town behind them on a course past Man Island to the Devil's Backbone. The day's dive itinerary would include visits to the Train Wreck, the Vanaheim, the Carnarvon and the Cienfuegos, all ships that had floundered on this treacherous coral reef in the past hundred years or so, and whose meager remains lie strewn across the sand between the towering coral heads. Not much remained, only a few rusted sections of the hulls and engines and in the case of the Train Wreck, three sets of wheels from a Union train that had been captured and sold by the Confederacy to a Cuban sugar plantation owner to raise money for the war effort.

It was a routine day of diving for them all as they were all quite experienced and capable divers. For some the reef was of more interest than the wrecks with its wonderful coral formations rising from the sea bottom to within a couple of feet of the water's surface, but for Hector it was a revelation to be able to swim in the very water that had changed the course of his life but it was hard for him to imagine the conditions that must have existed on that day when the ship went down because now the weather was calm and the sea tranquil. All that remained of the Cienfuegos was a piece of one of her boilers and a section of a drive shaft. Both remnants of what was once a proud passenger liner were partially buried in the sand forty feet below the surface of the ocean where they had lain for over a century. It wasn't much to see, yet to Hector it was an important connection to his past, and as he swam down to touch the scrap metal remains of the wreck, he felt an emotional pull that he could not explain. He imagined his grandparents floundering in the sea in this very spot and he felt tears forming in his eyes as he forced himself back to the surface. He ignored the concerned call of one of the dive masters as he swam ashore and collapsed on the beach. They might have been washed up right here, he thought, and this could well be the exact place where their feet felt the safety of terra firma after their frightening ordeal. He doubted if much had changed in a hundred years; a few trees had been toppled by hurricanes, the beach had been eroded by the tides, but all in all the scene was much the way it had been back then and this realization had a calming effect on Hector. His curiosity had been satiated by the reality of these surroundings, their very presence providing a tangible confirmation to what had always been an unclosed episode in his family's history. He could move ahead with a new perspective.

Juan Fernandez had booked passage on the Cienfuegos as a surprise for his new bride Consuello. It was to be their honeymoon. They were to be married in Havana in two weeks time and what better way could there be to start their new life together than a cruise on one of the newest and most luxurious liners that would take them to the West Indies, on to Charleston and back to Havana. Juan had business to complete in Puerto Rico and Santa Domingo and taking his new wife along on this trip would serve a dual purpose. Her beauty would impress his associates and their wives, and as a couple they would be welcomed into a society where he had been excluded for many years because he was a bachelor. It was important for his cigar manufacturing business that he find new distributors for his products and ones with influence, social standing and money. Juan had started his business in 1887 with one employee and very little capital. The cigars that they made each night would be sold the next day to the rich tourists that visited Havana, and slowly the business grew until he had twelve employees producing the finest cigars in all of Cuba. His reputation soared and the orders poured in. As such a young man to be operating a profitable endeavor, he became the target of every mother with an eligible daughter and his social status climbed to new heights. But Juan had his eye on Consuello.

She was the youngest daughter of one of his best customers who often accompanied her father to the cigar factory on her way to the private academy where she was being groomed to enter Havana's upper society. She was just seventeen when Juan first saw her as she sat waiting in the family carriage for her father to complete his purchases. It was a weekly ritual. The carriage arrived at a few minutes before nine in the morning outside of the factory, and while her father selected his cigars, Consuello would remain huddled inside. Juan was careful not to alert her father as he surreptitiously peeked out of his window hoping to catch a glimpse of the carriage's beautiful occupant. His heart almost stopped on one occasion when Consuello acknowledged his presence with what he could only interpret as the beginnings of a smile. A week later she smiled at him from the confines of the darkened interior of the carriage and actually waved her gloved hand in his direction. Juan contrived a way to meet her. His mother's dog had given birth to a litter of puppies and he brought one to his small office on the pretext that he needed a watch dog. The puppy was irresistible with sad brown eyes and ears that flopped almost to the ground as he scampered across the floor. The puppy would be the tool he would use to entice the pretty girl into his factory. On their next visit Juan made sure that the puppy was prominently displayed as the girl's father came to buy his cigars. After apologizing for the delay in filling his order, Juan suggested that he invite his daughter inside rather than leaving her waiting outside in the carriage. His ploy worked to perfection.

Up close she was even prettier than Juan had imagined. When she smiled at him as her father introduced them, he thought that his heart would burst. He had difficulty controlling his feelings, just breathing became a chore and his legs could hardly support him as he came forward to kiss her hand. Their eyes met for a second before her attention was diverted to the antics of the puppy, but in that brief moment Juan had the feeling that she had been anticipating this encounter as much as he had. On subsequent visits she always joined her father in the office to play with the little puppy, or at least that was the reason she gave. It was obvious to all the factory workers that their boss was infatuated with this pretty young girl who seemed to spend more and more time at their place of employment. Juan was thrilled by the frequency of her visits but was at a loss to find a way to meet with her socially. He knew that his background and lack of education would prevent him from being considered as a serious suitor by her family and even though her father was friendly and affable whenever they visited, Juan understood that this was only a mark of the man's social grace. He was astounded when he received an invitation to Consuello's eighteenth birthday party.

The invitation was on fine parchment with gold edging, hand written in wonderfully flowing script with the first letter of his name almost an inch in height. He wondered if Consuello had taken extra care in the writing of his name or if in fact she had even written the invitation herself. The event was to take place on the following Saturday evening at her home. Dress was to be formal. Juan was confident in himself and although he was thrilled and surprised to have been invited he was not daunted by the enormity of the occasion. His only concern was the selection of a suitable gift. He knew that she would probably receive many expensive trinkets, jewelry, colognes and other quite proper tokens of her friends' and admirers' respect. He also knew that he could not afford to compete with her other suitors, which he assumed would be present in large numbers. He needed a unique gift. A gift that she would treasure. He wrote a poem that expressed his adoration for her. It was a bold but calculated move that could either be received with gratitude or a move that could result in the termination of their brief friendship. He attached the poem to the jeweled collar of the puppy that he had decided to give her for her birthday.

He dressed with extra care in the new formal suit that he had been fitted for earlier in the week and with the newly shampooed puppy under his arm, he walked up to the front door of Consuello's home. He was somewhat surprised to discover that he was the first to arrive, because he had purposely tried to arrive a half an hour after the time given on the invitation. There were no carriages in the driveway, no cabbies waiting and no sounds of music coming from inside the imposing house.

Juan was to be the only guest at Consuello's eighteenth birthday. The puppy was an immediate hit, and as if on demand it licked Consuello's face with its warm pink tongue. The poem which was meant to be a very private communication between the two young friends was read aloud for both her parents to hear, and for the first time in his life Juan blushed. His embarrassment was relieved when Consuello's father placed his arm around Juan's shoulder in a fatherly gesture and escorted him to the dining table which had only four settings.

"This was my daughter's idea," he stated. "She wanted only you as her guest and my daughter's happiness is very important to me."

"I don't know what to say," Juan stammered.

"It's very obvious to me that you are enamored with Consuello and she talks of nothing else but you; it would be wrong and fruitless of me to stand in the way of this mutual adoration, so you have my blessing to court my daughter. Please don't hurt her."

"Thank you, sir," was all Juan could say.

Their courtship started slowly, as neither of them had any prior experience in matters of the heart, but their love for each other soon precluded any rules they may have thought had been written on the subject. Three months later they went together to ask Consuello's father for his permission to allow them to be married, and while her mother wept tears of joy, he shook Juan's hand and welcomed him as a son. And now just twelve months later he was making secret arrangements for their honeymoon.

The shipping agent had provided Juan with a sketch of the cabin arrangement of the Cienfuegos which showed the location of each one of its fifty-four cabins. Most were on the main deck, but two were located on the bridge deck forward of the navigation center. These were usually reserved for the owner's guests explained the agent, but on this trip one of them would be empty and available. Cabin number two would be perfect for the newlyweds.

Their wedding had a storybook quality to it. Juan was like a handsome prince in his tuxedo and Consuello was as pretty as any fairytale princess in her long white dress with its lace veil that had been worn by both her mother and grandmother at both of their weddings. The weather cooperated to make the day perfect and the exuberant guests insisted on accompanying the newlywed couple to the ship to see them off on their voyage. The captain of the ship welcomed them on board and invited them to dine with him later that evening as he personally escorted them to cabin number two where several bouquets of flowers and a complimentary bottle of champagne were waiting. As the ship cast off its dock lines Consuello and Juan joined the rest of the passengers at the ship's rail to wave a final goodbye to the many well-wishers that crowded the quay side. A small brass band played a lively tune as hundreds of balloons were sent into the sky to the shrieks of delight of the crowd. Coincidentally this was also the maiden voyage of the Cienfuegos from Havana and a proud addition to the fleet of ships operated by the Ward Line Steamship company of New York. She was two hundred feet in length and powered by a single steam powered engine driven by two boilers through a main drive shaft that turned a seventy-two inch propeller. The advent of steam ships had changed the itinerary of the shipping industry by allowing ships to make faster passages to their destinations with no regard to the strength or direction of the wind. The Cienfuegos did carry two sails, one forward and one aft to provide a dampening effect to the ocean swells and to make the passage more comfortable for its passengers, but these sails could not be used to drive the ship. In her day, a hundred and ten years ago, she was considered to be the height of luxury and safety, but by today's standards she was crude, uncomfortable and questionably seaworthy. Her passage was navigated by the captain and first mate using star sights at night and sun observations during the day, if the sun shone. She was isolated from other ships and from land and at the mercy of the weather. On board the cabins were dark and damp with only oil lamps to read by or to negotiate one's way through the dim corridors of the ship, and when the seas became rough the passengers were often ordered to their cabins and the oil lamps extinguished for fear of fire. And this was a 'first class' voyage.

But to Juan and Consuello it was romantic, relaxing and exhilarating. As they paraded around the decks they were greeted by the other passengers and invited for card games, drinks, a smoke with the men for Juan and a chit chat with the women for Consuello. When it was discovered that Juan was the manufacturer of the cigars that many of the men smoked, his status soared and he was asked if he required any investors or partners in his company. He knew then that his decision to expand his business into other Caribbean countries was the right one and that the expense of the trip would pay dividends in the future. As much as they enjoyed the company of the other passengers, it was the time that they spent alone that they relished. In the dimly lit cabin with the ship gently rolling and pitching, they made tender love every night until they fell asleep wrapped in each others arms.

If Consuello was a hit in Santa Domingo then she was a triumph in San Juan. Her new husband could not have been more proud of her as he watched how she was adored by both men and women at every function they attended. How could he have been so lucky, he asked himself as she smiled at him with such love in her eyes, even as she was surrounded by dozens of admirers?

The time passed by so quickly and the new customers Juan had encountered would provide his business with so many orders for cigars that he would need to expand once again. It was with a feeling of apprehension that he confided to Consuello his concern over the success of the trip and the potential size of the increase in business and the difficulties he knew that he would face in the expansion of his company. She reassured him with a grin of confidence and laughed at his concerns.

"Not many young men are as fortunate as you to have such problems to face. I know that you'll find a way to overcome them. Isn't this the reason that we came?"

She was right, of course, thought Juan, "I will find a way."

The Cienfuegos departed from San Juan with a full cargo of rice, a full complement of passengers, some replacing those who had chosen to remain on shore for a longer stay, and an increased number of crew who would be required on the long non-stop voyage to Nassau where they would stay overnight before embarking to Charleston. The Captain explained during dinner, in response to a question from Juan, that the ship would travel east of the Bahamas, approaching the coast of Eleuthera before turning west through the deep water passage to Nassau. The trip was to take nine days if the weather remained favourable.

Even today this route is followed by many modern cruise ships that journey to the eastern Caribbean. They can easily be observed from the north shore of Spanish Wells, as they pass by five or six miles offshore. Today's vessels have the luxury of up-to-date weather information, accurate navigation technology and constant radio contact with other ships. It wasn't this way back in 1895.

Six days after leaving Puerto Rico a drop in barometric pressure was reported to the Captain by the mate, it continued to drop over the next twenty-four hours, alerting the crew to an impending storm. By the time the ship turned westwards towards Nassau the wind had increased to over sixty knots and the seas were piling up to a height of twelve to fourteen feet. The Captain had an uneasy feeling that the rapid change in pressure and wind speed could easily be the beginning of an onslaught by a hurricane. He ordered all the passengers to their cabins, where they were told to remain until the storm passed. He ordered that all lamps be extinguished and loose bags and furniture be secured; he also advised some of the male passengers to take sufficient rope with them to their cabins to tie themselves and their wives to the beds to avoid being thrown around. The weather quickly worsened. Juan tried to allay Consuello's fears as he fastened everything that could move in their cabin with the ropes that the Captain had provided, but when he suggested that they tie themselves to the bed, she balked at the idea, saying that she needed to be able to move in the advent of a disaster. The crew fastened boards called 'dead lights' over the windows, shutting out the light and plunging the interior of the cabin into total darkness. It was frightening in the darkness as the two young honeymooners clung to each other while listening to the constant throbbing of the engine, the howling of the wind and the crashing of the waves. They had no way of knowing if it was day or night, whether the ship had remained on course or if the worst of the storm had passed. They tried to sleep as they clung to each other, but it was impossible. The shear exertion of preventing themselves from being thrown across the cabin began to take its toll on Consuello, she began to sob and several times she screamed as the ship buried itself in the waves and seemed to be sinking, but each time the forward motion brought her up.

It was sometime during the night that the comforting throbbing of the engine stopped.

The motion of the ship changed dramatically as she came broadside to huge waves. The ship rolled so violently that it became impossible for the passengers to remain either on their feet or attached to the cabin's interior furnishings as everything was thrown about; even previously secured items were wrenched from their mountings. Juan and Consuello's cabin was awash with sea water as the waves washed over the decks and flooded everything in their path. The loud bellowing of the claxton horn was the signal for abandoning ship and Consuello was the first to hear it above the deafening noise of the hurricane. As Juan gathered together their papers and valuables and stuffed them into his pocket, Consuello grabbed the two canvas life preservers from the rack above the cabin door. They tied their hats securely onto their heads and cautiously open the door on the leeside of the cabin. The wind tore at their clothes as the water sloshed over their feet; it was impossible to even shout over the terrifying noise and all that Juan could do was to hold on tightly to the rail with one hand while making sure that he held onto Consuello with his other. The First Mate, who had tied himself to the ship's main stairway to avoid being swept overboard, saw them approaching and went to help them. He yelled into Juan's ear telling him to hurry into one of the four wooden lifeboats that had been launched.

"Where are we?" shouted Juan.

"Off the north coast of Eleuthera," bellowed the First Mate. "It's close to high tide right now, it maybe high enough that the lifeboat will clear the reef. Just pray."

The small lifeboat had almost forty passengers and crew crammed into her. Two crew members manned the oars while a third handled the tiller. All they could do was to keep the boat from capsizing as it was hurled across the coral reef towards the shore. Moments later they heard the unmistakable sound of the steel hulled ship being pounded onto the reef as they all prayed silently for their survival.

Eli Pinder was securing his Father's wagon and horses on their farm on North Eleuthera when he heard the long blasts of the ship's horn. Eli was only fourteen but knew from experience that a ship was in trouble and floundering on the Devil's Backbone. He also knew that there was nothing anyone could do to help until the storm had abated; what he didn't know was that the ship was a passenger ship with almost two hundred passengers and crew on board.

Eli lived in the town of Spanish Wells with his Mother and Father but spent most of his time tending the farm on Eleuthera that was a part of the commonage property deeded to the people of the town by Queen Victoria in 1842. He sailed a small lateen-rigged dinghy across the shallow water between Spanish Wells and the mainland each day usually returning at dusk. He knew his only chance of reaching his home to tell the people of the town of the plight of the ship, was to wait until the eye of the hurricane was directly overhead. He just hoped that he would make it in the brief time that the calm prevailed because if he didn't the wind would capsize his small boat and sweep him out to sea. As if by magic the sun came out and the wind stopped blowing as Eli launched his boat and began his journey across to Spanish Wells. As he reached the eastern most point of the town the wind began to blow from the south pushing a wall of water into the narrow creek between Charles Island and St. George's Island which formed the protected harbour of Spanish Wells. Eli hurriedly secured his boat and ran from the storm to his house.

"There's a ship on the reef," he shouted as he ran. "I heard the ship's horn blasting," he told his Father when he reached home.

"Ain't nothin' we can do 'til this wind dies," his father commented.

"There could be people in trouble," said his wife with genuine concern in her voice. "We'll need to organize a rescue party."

"All in good time. Right now we're stayin' put!"

Spanish Wells in 1895 had a population of only 140 souls. They lived in small houses at the eastern end of the island with nothing west of what is now the Batelco office. The Methodist church, now part of the site of Ronald's Service Centre, was at the center of their lives and it was to the church that Eli's mother, against her better judgment and her husband's threats, made her way by dodging between the houses as the wind gusted and whipped its path through the town. She knew that many families were seeking shelter in the church and she was determined to alert them to the disaster and begin organizing the rescue. There was no time to waste.

It was four hours later that the first group of rescuers braved the elements in their small sail boats and arrived at Gun Point on the main land of Eleuthera. It was another hour before they arrived at the north coast to find debris strewn along the beach and the surf pounding flotsam into pieces as it continued to rage. There was no sign of any survivors. The town's people found the remains of four life boats, two were being hurled against the rocks by the storm, but two had been pulled high onto the beach beyond the high water line. Somebody had dragged the heavy boats to safety.

"Search the cave," yelled Eli's Father above the noise of the surf. "If they've a brain in their heads it's where they'll be!"

They found evidence that people had been along the path to the cave; pieces of dresses caught on the Kantaberry bushes, lost leather shoes, discarded hats and scarves and broken suitcases.

It was Eli, running ahead to the Preacher's Cave, who found them first. Actually he heard them before he reached the cave. They were singing. As the group of Spanish Wells fishermen and their wives followed Eli into the cave, they were overwhelmed by the emotional out-pouring of the shipwreck survivors. It didn't matter that they were total strangers, it didn't matter that they couldn't understand each others language, it didn't matter that these people were wealthy educated merchants and their families and the rescuers just simple folk from a fishing village, nor did it matter that they were Catholic while the local people were Methodists. The enormity of the occasion prompted a spontaneous reaction from everyone as they hugged each other and clasped each others hands. Slowly they all fell to their knees and prayed together in their own language but to a common listener.

The tears streamed uncontrollably from Consuello's eyes as she hugged Eli's Mother in a long embrace, while Juan clung to Eli's Father's hand as he hurled a barrage of questions at him. Only a handful of the Cubans spoke English and none of them fluently. Consuello knew a little English from her days in the Academy and she was able to understand enough to learn where they were and what the prospects of returning to Cuba were. The Captain tried to explain that they needed to reach Nassau to be able to send a message informing the ship's owners of the disaster and to the families of the passengers to let them know that no lives had been lost. There were four passengers and one crew member who needed medical attention and Eli and his two friends were dispatched to the farms to collect the three wagons that comprised the total available transportation. It was Eli's Father who made a quick assessment of the situation. He counted the survivors in the cave, and whispered quietly to his wife in a voice that was overheard by several people adjacent to him, that there were more of them than the total population of Spanish Wells.

"How will we feed them?' he asked.

"We'll manage," replied his wife.

"And where will they sleep?"

"Sshh," she cautioned. "We'll manage."

"But how? There's more of them than us!"

And somehow they did manage. The transfer of all the survivors from the cave by farm wagon, then by small boats to Spanish Wells took three days to complete. Salvaging the cargo of rice from the wrecked ship took almost two weeks and the collection of pieces of wreckage and lost personal belongings went on for months.

Derek Hawkins

The Methodist church was converted into a dormitory for the Captain and his crew, while most of the passengers billeted with the local towns-people in their small houses. As the weather steadily improved, many of the local fishing boats were commandeered to ferry the passengers to Nassau. Finally they were all gone. Consuello and Juan were the last to leave and even though they were eager to return to their home, they could hardly tear themselves away from Eli's family. The two women hugged each other and cried, while the men shook hands and slapped each other on the back. Neither could find the words to express their feelings, but they both knew that their lives had been enriched by their meeting. They doubted that they would ever meet again.

Hector Fernandez arrived in Spanish Wells on the day after he had dived on the wreck of the Cienfuegos. He still had the vision in his head of the surf, the beach and the cave he had visited after learning that this was the place that had provided a sanctuary for his great grandparents. He was looking for the family of Eli Pinder. The diary that his great grandmother kept over a hundred years ago, described how young Eli, had had a major role in the rescue and the eventual repatriation of the Cuban passengers, and in whose modest home they had found shelter for several weeks after the shipwreck. Hector hoped to find a direct descendent of Eli's, a son or daughter perhaps or at least a family member who could remember their infamous ancestor. It was at the Post Office that he encountered his first hurdle, when following his inquiry into the family of Eli Pinder, he was informed that almost one third of the town's population bore the surname of Pinder.

At the suggestion of the attractive girl behind the counter at the Post Office, Hector sought out Gregory Pinder.

"He's been around for a long time," she commented, "and if anyone can remember, 'e will."

He located Gregory Pinder outside Ronald's Service Centre, where he was engaged in a deep meaningful conversation with what must have been the most intellectual segment of the population. He was surrounded by a collection of weather-beaten senior citizens whose faces bore the marks of many years at sea and whose average age appeared to be close to seventy five. Hector calculated that if Eli had been a mere boy in 1895, maybe ten years old or so, he would most likely have lived until around the time of the second world war, and any offspring he may have conceived would be close to sixty today. He was surprised when, in response to his questions, he was told by Gregory that he had no recollection of an Eli Pinder.

Hector stuck his hands in the pockets of his shorts and, with a defeated look on his face, he ambled along the waterfront past Abner's, the Supermarket and the Boatyard, while he tried to think of a new tactic to discover the whereabouts of the elusive Eli. He decided to check the cemetery, hoping that maybe he'd find a stone that mentioned Eli's name, devoted son of Eli or beloved daughter of Eli, anything that could provide a clue to this man. His search was fruitless. Not wanting to admit defeat, Hector headed west through town to the Methodist Church hoping that there he might uncover an old town record that contained the name Eli, only to be told by the young Reverend that all the church records had been lost during a fire before the new church had been built. He had reached an impasse; there was no choice but to return home.

An old man was slowly raking leaves from the church lawn as Hector passed by on his way back to catch the Ferry to Harbour Island. The old man was smoking a cigar, and its fragrance stopped Hector in his tracks. It was not possible for anyone to be able to correctly identify the brand of cigar from its odour, but it was possible for an expert like Hector to distinguish an expensive cigar from a cheap one. The cigar that the old man had stuck in his mouth was definitely expensive.

"Excuse me," Hector called.

The old man looked up from his raking to see who was calling; as he did he emitted a cloud of cigar smoke that reconfirmed Hector's initial appraisal of the quality of the cigar that the man was smoking.

"I'd like to ask you a question," Hector continued.

"Are yer lost?"

"No, I know where I am. It's your cigar."

The old man looked at his cigar as if it was a smoking firecracker.

"Is it gonna explode?" he asked.

"No, it's nothing like that. I'd like to ask you where it came from."

After a moment the old man responded. He didn't know why this young man wanted to know the origin of his cigar but he was polite enough to furnish him with the answer.

"From my Granny," he replied.

"She smokes cigars?" Hector asked incredulously.

He had calculated that the old man must be close to sixty. Just to have a Granny was remarkable in itself, yet alone one who smoked cigars. She'd have to be close to a hundred years old.

The old man chucked at the suggestion.

"Lord no," he laughed. "She hates the smell of 'em."

He went on to explain.

"She receives a big box of 'em every Christmas from Cuba. Bin gettin' 'em for years now."

Hector introduced himself to the old man, explaining to him that he was from Cuba and he manufactured cigars.

"Could I ask your name, sir?" Hector inquired.

"Elijah Albury," he answered proudly.

"I'd like to meet your Granny."

"She don't go out, no more," Elijah said.

"Then please take me to meet her," Hector pleaded.

After a considerable amount of persuasion on Hector's part, Elijah agreed to let him accompany him to the little house where he lived with his Granny. He made one stipulation. If Granny refused to see him, he must leave without any fuss and be on his way. Hector sat in an old rocker on the canted porch while Elijah conversed with Granny. He suspected that the cigars were from his own factory in Cuba, but by whom and why they were being sent to the Bahamas to an old lady was beyond him. There had to be a link of some kind to Eli and his great grandparents. Several minutes passed before Elijah reappeared with what must have been the closest thing to a smile on his wrinkled face.

"She'll see yer for a bit," he declared with considerable surprise in his voice. "Follow me."

He led Hector into the dimly lit, low-ceiling abode where the two of them lived. Hector was sure that he was the first visitor they had allowed into the house for ages. The house was dark and smelled musty and stale. Granny was seated at the kitchen table eating an apple that she had peeled with an old sharp knife; he watched for a moment as she chewed each little piece a hundred times with the couple of teeth that remained in her mouth. He sat down opposite her and waited for her to finish the apple. Twenty minutes passed before she looked up at him and spoke to him.

"You makes them ceegars?" she asked him.

"Yes I do. In Cuba in a factory that I inherited from my great grandfather".

"So," she commented.

"I'm wondering who sends them to you."

"Not sure who," she said "but they bin coming for more than a hundred years, addressed to my father. I gives 'em to the boy 'ere."

The boy she indicated was Elijah.

"Never knowed my father" she rambled on without being prompted. "He died the same year as I was born, 1903; he would have bin eighteen then."

"Was your father named Eli?" Hector asked.

"That's 'im," she confirmed "Eli Pinder. God rest 'is soul."

Hector told her the story of the shipwreck and the heroic role that Eli and his family had played in rescuing the passengers and how they had become friends with his ancestors.

"I heard tell somethin' about it, but it 'appened years before I was born. I do remember eatin' the rice though" she grinned. "Never had to buy any rice for forty years."

Hector and Elijah both laughed in unison at the joke.

"It were true," she chastised them, "it weren't no joke."

The Kantaberry Tales

Hector thought for a moment of this discovery that he had made. He was talking to Eli's daughter, who by his reckoning must be over a hundred years old, and who was a tangible link to his great grandparents. He had accomplished his mission and a warm glow of satisfaction spread through him as he sat in awe of the old lady, who in fact looked younger than her grandson. He watched as she walked into the small kitchen where she collected a bottle from the refrigerator and two glasses from the kitchen counter. She poured the purple liquid from the bottle into the two glasses and offered one to Hector.

"Ere," she said "drink this."

"What is it?" he asked as he took the glass from her and held it under his nose.

"Kantaberry juice," she stated "I drink a glass of it everyday of my life. Try it. It'll help keep your pecker up."

It tasted like Welch's grape juice to Hector, but if it kept his pecker up and contributed to a long life, then he had nothing to lose.

When Hector returned to Cuba three days later he inquired into the shipments of cigars to the Bahamas. There was no record of any such shipments in the company's records. Further in depth inquiries into the sale of these particular cigars by the box full at Christmas time, led him to one of the most prestigious law firms in Havana, where he discovered it had been his great grandmother Consuello who had instructed her family's lawyer to send the cigars each year to Eli. The shipments had been sent regularly for a hundred and nine years and Hector could see no reason to halt them now.

He created two knew brands of cigars to be added to his company's inventory. The first he called Panatela Cigillia, a derivation of the word Cigillian. Even today the inhabitants of Spanish Wells refer to themselves as Cigillians, a word in itself derived from the pre Columbian Lucayan Indian word Sigatoo. The second brand he named Corona Eleuthera. Look for them both in the stores the next time you visit this unique part of the world, and while you are enjoying their aroma give a thought to the many families who were responsible for their manufacture.

THE DROP

Frankie Albury had had a 'Murphy's Law' day. Everything that could go wrong, did. It started early in the morning when his newly born baby had begun to cry without any let up, then the usually well-behaved dog had soiled the new carpet in the living room, then the fish tank had somehow sprung a leak depositing twelve gallons of salt water and eight damselfish onto the same carpet, and all this after his wife had decided to go home to her mother.

He yelled at the dog, dumped the fish down the toilet, tried to pacify his child and cursed under his breath at his wife. Fortunately for the child, the dog and the fish his actions were direct and orderly at this time of the morning. Had it been later in the day he could have quite easily yelled at the child, tried to pacify the fish, cursed at the dog and dumped his wife down the toilet.

He called over to his Mother-in law's house to speak with his wife, only to be told that she couldn't come to the phone and that if could have, she wouldn't. Frankie slammed the phone down and put his hands over his ears to try to shut out the heart wrenching cries of the baby. The child needed its mother. Against his better judgment he carried the screaming child to the car and deposited her in the back seat, he smashed his head on the door strut as he maneuvered the baby's basket into a safe place and then he dropped the keys down between the front seats into a concealed place designed especially by General Motors as a place where retrieving the keys would be almost impossible. The baby continued to scream. He caught his neighbor watching and laughing from behind the curtains of her window; he was tempted to give her the finger but checked his anger just in time and only waved his hand. He backed out of the garage over his neighbor's son's bicycle that had been discarded in his driveway. He clipped the fence with the front fender as he tried to feed the baby a bottle while driving with one hand.

"She isn't 'ere," replied his wife's Father in response to Frankie's question as to the whereabouts of his wife.

"Where the devil is she?"

"Gone to Briland wiv the missus," he stated. "They caught the Bo Hengy this morning, won't be back 'til four thirty."

Frankie knew that there was no point in asking his Father-in-law to look after his grandchild so that he could go to work, because the family had made it very clear to him that he wasn't good enough for their daughter and would never be welcomed into their house. Even the plaintive cries from the back seat failed to soften the old man's heart and only solicited a remark that accused Frankie of neglecting the child. He walked back down the driveway to the car only to find that the front tire was flat. What else could go wrong? It was almost noon by the time he'd fixed the tire and arrived back home with the baby finally sleeping peacefully in its basket. He left the engine running in the hope that the baby would continue to sleep. He wound down the window to provide some circulation of air in the car's interior as he felt a pang of guilt for leaving the child unattended in the car. He attempted to call his boss to tell him that he wouldn't be in to work but the telephone only crackled when he tried to make the call. The phones had been acting strangely ever since the last hurricane; it was an annual problem in the area with some subscribers still without service after several months. He tried the call again. This time he heard a voice, two voices actually. He could hear both sides of a confidential conversation. His first reaction was to hang up, but his curiosity had been aroused, so he listened.

Derek Hawkins

"The contact will be seated at table four in the Snack Bar at eleven-thirty," said the first voice.

"Who is he?" the second asked.

"I've no idea. What does it matter anyway? He doesn't know you and you don't know him."

"Its two hours drive from here. I can't make it".

"Then send somebody in your place; we're just trying to repay you for all the good work you've done for us."

"I understand but it's impossible."

"Well, he'll be there as arranged this morning but he won't wait. His instructions are clear on that."

"Tell me again what I'm supposed to do."

"You put a thousand dollars into a Styrofoam cup, sit down opposite him at his table, he takes your cup and exchanges it for his. Then he leaves. You wait for a couple of minutes, take his cup and leave. Inside of the cup is a small package with a name and address of someone in Nassau. You deliver the package and collect ten thousand dollars for it. The money is yours to keep!"

"That's it? Nobody knows anything?"

The Kantaberry Tales

"Right, it's that simple."

"What happens if I don't show, and I can't find anyone to be there in my place?"

"He'll just leave and set it up for another time."

"That'll be better for me."

The phone connection crackled again and ended.

It must be some sort of drug deal payoff, thought Frankie. Two hours away could only be from Rock Sound or some place in South Eleuthera. The lure of making nine thousand dollars for a trip to Nassau was a tremendous temptation.

It's just about full proof, he conjectured. They said that the man didn't know them, so he wouldn't know me either, if I went in his place. And I'm just delivering a package, just like FedEx or the post office; they do it every day and they don't have to know what's inside.

He had less than an hour to find a thousand dollars and to keep the appointment.

Remembering that he had left his baby unattended in the car, he rushed out of the house to check, only to find that she was still sound asleep. Thank God for small mercies he mumbled to himself as his gunned the engine and took off to his friend Tommy's house.

"I have to come up with a thousand dollars; it's for the baby. I'm going to Nassau this afternoon. To the hospital," he lied.

"Put it on your credit card. You can get cash from the new ATM machine at the bank," suggested Tommy.

"I can only get three hundred."

"Then use more than one card."

"I only have one. Will you lend me yours? I'll pay you back tomorrow."

Tommy agreed to lend his friend the money, so the two of them drove to the bank and collected the thousand dollars by using three credit cards in the machine.

It was now eleven-twenty.

Frankie bought a jumbo coke in a Styrofoam cup from The Gap and hurried to the Snack Bar to keep the appointment. As he pulled to a stop outside the waterfront café he could hear his heart pounding. He willed himself to be brave and to act normally. He hoisted the baby from the baby seat and carried her with him into the Snack Bar. There was a stranger seated at table four. He walked over to the table placed his cup on the glass table top and sat down. The man's eyes never made contact with Frankie's as he picked up the cup and said,

"Here take this table. I was just leaving."

And that was it. He was gone with the money in the cup.

Frankie waited for a minute or two before making an excuse to the hovering waitress that he had forgotten something and had to leave. He picked up the replacement cup and exited the café. He drove to the eastern end of the island, where he parked the car and opened the cup. He extracted a small package that measured no more than four inches long and was wrapped neatly in brown paper with the name Julian Trelawny printed in bold letters on a name tag. There was an address on Village Road included.

He felt like a criminal as he drove home. He was sure that the small package contained enough cocaine or heroin to land him in jail for the rest of his life if he was apprehended. His palms were wet on the steering wheel and he was having trouble breathing. Every car that passed posed a threat and he refrained from waving as was his normal daily routine because he didn't trust in his ability to drive safely with just one shaking hand. He pulled into his driveway, carefully avoiding any eye contact with his nosey neighbor, lifted his daughter from her seat and carried both her and the little package into the house. He was thankful for the fact that most of the hurricane shutters were still covering the windows as they provided a secure and safe atmosphere from which he gained a certain degree of comfort by just knowing that no one could possibly see inside.

He examined the package, turning it over and over in his hands and wondering who Julian Trelawny might be. Was he a middle man, a distributor, a consumer or just an innocent courier as he was? His suspicions about the contents of the package were confirmed when he discovered a deposit of white powder on his fingers. He put his fingers to his nose to check if the white powder smelled like cocaine or heroin, not that he would have known how either substance smelled. He was a little disappointed to find that it smelled like talcum powder, but he conjectured that he was dealing with professionals and that they had probably devised a technology to make the drugs smell like talcum powder to avoid detection from those expert sniffing dogs that he had seen on Sixty Minutes.

He looked at the back of the name tag and noticed two words scrawled in blue ink. AFTER TEN. Could it be a message from Trelawny or was it an old tag that had been used and the message was unrelated to this package drop? If the delivery was to be made in the evening he would have to stay overnight in Nassau. A complication that he hadn't counted on. The prospect of collecting ten thousand dollars was reason enough for Frankie to decide to pack an overnight bag. He'd come up with a plausible explanation to his wife after he had the money when she'd be in a more receptive frame of mind. His plan was beginning to take shape. He'd board the Bo Hengy at four thirty and transfer the baby to his wife as she returned from Brilland. He was hoping that the Bo Hengy's brief stop in Spanish Wells would be extra brief today, thus precluding his wife from asking too many questions. He fed the baby, changed her diaper, then poured himself a stiff drink of vodka and kantaberry juice, found an overnight bag in his closet into which he packed a spare shirt, some underwear and his toilet articles in preparation for the trip.

Frankie was starting to feel better. The day's events had continued to improve as the day had passed and he was now on the verge of obtaining a chunk of cash that would help to provide many of the things that his new family needed. He was convinced that his wife's contempt for him would dissipate when she learned of his enterprising ingenuity and his dogged determination to provide for their daughter.

His elevated mood was suddenly deflated as he heard a hard rapping on his front door.

"Who's there?" he called out nervously.

He was imagining the stranger from the Snack Bar lurking outside after he had obviously followed him home.

"It's me," yelled Tommy. "How come your door's locked?"

Frankie hurried to the door and unlocked the three sliding bolts that secured the door. Tommy waited patiently outside listening to his friend opening up the door.

"What are you hiding in here that you need three locks on your door? And why do you have them fastened in the daytime?"

"I don't want the dog to run off!"

"That old dog can hardly run anyway and one lock would be plenty for him. You're up to something!"

"Don't be stupid Tommy. You know I'm too dumb to be up to anything!"

Frankie proceeded to feed the baby while Tommy looked around the house for some evidence to confirm his suspicion that Frankie was up to something. He rummaged through the open overnight back and found the gun.

"What's this?" he pronounced as he waved the pistol in his hand.

"I'm staying over in Nassau and I figured I might need it."

"You must be joking," Tommy exclaimed. "If they find you with a gun they'll lock you up and throw away the key. Now I know you're up to something!"

"Please don't ask any more questions. I can't tell you what I'm doing, but I'll tell you when I come home."

"Are you in trouble?" Tommy asked.

"I don't think so, but I have to meet someone in Nassau and I don't know what the outcome might be. I'll just feel safer with the gun in my pocket."

"Is it loaded?"

"No, course not. I don't have a license."

"I wish you'd leave it at home. Pointing an unloaded gun at somebody can get you killed."

"I know. I'm sure I won't really need it."

By four o'clock they had consumed three drinks each and Frankie was feeling no pain. Tommy had agreed to drive him to the ferry dock along with the baby and to drive Frankie's wife back to their house. They reached the dock just as the boat came into view. There were only a handful of passengers boarding the vessel and only Frankie's wife and her Mother disembarking. They passed briefly on the gangway where

Frankie transferred the baby into its Mother's arms and in response to her surprised questions, Frankie promised to call her later from Nassau.

A black German shepherd sniffed at his carryon bag as Frankie searched for a seat away from the other passengers.

"What have you got in there, hamburger meat?" asked the dog's owner with a laugh.

"No," replied Frankie with a false grin. "Its some of my Mother's sausage rolls."

It was seven o'clock by the time Frankie found a taxi to take him to his hotel. He had three hours to kill. He was too nervous to eat, too hung over to have another drink and too scared to walk the streets. He just sat on the bed in his poorly furnished room and thought about how he would spend his newfound wealth.

The room at the front of their house would be converted into a nursery with pretty girlish wallpaper, pink frilly curtains and a crib with a pink canopy. He'd buy her a golden brush for her hair like the one his mother used to have and a doll that cried real tears. He'd get her all the things that he had never been able to afford, all the things that his wife had told him that they had to buy and that if he couldn't she'd find somebody that could.

He found a pad of paper in the bedside table next to the Gideon Bible and started to make a list. If he stayed an extra day he would have time to go shopping and return home with his arms full of gifts rather than just the money. Frankie liked that idea.

He decided to call home to let his wife know that he wouldn't be home until the day after tomorrow. He settled back onto the bed with the telephone cradled into his shoulder feeling euphoric and excited by his plan. He was bursting to tell his wife the good news, but decided to play it cool and let her rant and rave for a while before dispelling her anger.

She took a while to answer, so long in fact that Frankie became concerned that she wasn't home and that just maybe she had decided to take this opportunity that his absence had provided to leave him for good. He emitted an audible sigh of relief when she finally answered.

"Hi honey," he said, "it's just me. I thought for a moment that you weren't home."

"Where else would I be?" she answered coolly.

"What are you doing?"

"I was watching television. ZNS news. They were reporting the details of a scam that's been going on right here in Spanish

Wells and other places in Eleuthera. These people evidently interrupt telephone conversations to make it sound as though the listener is hearing a confidential conversation by mistake. They play a tape setting up a meeting, complete with locations and times and they get these gullible fools to hand over a thousand dollars to them on the promise that they'll collect a big payoff when they deliver a package of talcum powder. The reporter said that they were conning at least ten people every week. Can you imagine how stupid some people must be?"

Frankie did not respond.

"Hello. Are you still there?" she called over and over again before she finally hung up.

SAFE SEX

In their senior year at the Spanish Wells All Age School the students were introduced to sex education. It was a mandatory subject, part of the curriculum incorporated into the 'new wave' of education policy directed by the Central Board of Education.

Miss Gibbons was selected by the principal to be the teacher of this new controversial subject and it was her unenviable task to try to teach the senior class the ins and outs of sex. The selection of Miss Gibbons was in itself controversial. She was unmarried, close to retirement age and a former teacher at an all girl's Catholic school, hardly, in the opinion of the majority of the students and their parents, the qualifications required for a lecturer on sex education. But as it was pointed out by the Principal in her defense, most teachers that teach geography have never visited the countries that they were required to teach about.

The news was received with mixed reactions by the parents of those students who would be required to be instructed in sex education. Many thought that this was a topic to be avoided at all costs or a topic that was the responsibility of the church or the parents. Some welcomed the news as a step forward and some were relieved to know that they were no longer required to tackle the subject at home. Others were heard to remark that it was about time as the kids were receiving an education from the wrong sources, while some expressed their curiosity about the homework needs. Several fathers questioned the appointment of Miss Gibbons as the teacher with such statements as 'What does she know about sex, she's an old maid' or 'When did she learn all this stuff'.

Emily Pinder's parents welcomed the news with enthusiasm. Their daughter was one of the prettiest and well-developed girls in the senior class and at fifteen was receiving adoring looks from many of her male peers. Her safety and well-being were a constant cause of disagreement between her parents, who continually argued about the time she had to be home, the places she was allowed to go, the friends she was allowed to have over and the boys that she was allowed to 'date'. They lived in constant fear that she would be tempted to experiment with sex and wind up pregnant. On several occasions their well-intentioned over protectiveness had resulted in Emily's tearful exit from the dinner table as Emily had been wrongfully accused of some act that her parents thought was inappropriate. If only they had known, Emily already knew far more about sex than either of her parents and, as she often reminded them she was far too smart to let anything happen to her.

At the very first class Miss Gibbons presided over each student was handed a condom as they entered the classroom. For most, if not all, it was the first that they had handled and many had a nervous reaction to the product. Several refused to even touch the packet let alone its contents; others blew them up like balloons and let them fly around the room, while some carefully secreted them in their pockets for use at a later date. The news of this brazen classroom display was protested loudly and clearly by the majority of the parents with the demand for Miss Gibbons' resignation being urged by the Principal. But Miss Gibbons stayed and the sex education classes continued. During the course of the next few weeks the students learned about sexually transmitted diseases, their causes and prevention, the use of birth control devices for both males and females, and they were overwhelmed by the staggering amount of statistical data they had to read relating to the population explosion. The class was a success with all the students and with the exception of a few of the most conservative, an unequivocal success with the parents. Each of the students took away from the lectures at least one vital piece of information that could well have a life-altering effect upon them. For Emily it was the realization that there was no cure for AIDS, that just one experience could be disastrous and that without adequate protection she would be literally risking her life. It was a scary thought.

Emily met Jack at Easter. She met him in Orlando while she was on a senior class trip. Jack was eighteen, cute and fun. Her girlfriends were all captivated by him and would have quickly jumped into her shoes given half a chance, but it was Emily that Jack fancied. He made no bones about it, following her wherever she went, buying her little souvenirs and gifts and telephoning her each night at the hotel. Emily was flattered by his attention and without much encouragement from her friends she agreed to a one-on-one date with him. It was Jack's intention to get her away from her friends so that he could seduce her. He wasn't subtle about it, reminding her that she was only in town for a few days and that they couldn't waste any time with preliminaries. Their evening together was an unmitigated disaster. He tried to get Emily drunk but only succeeded in becoming drunk himself. His hands wandered out-of-control over her whenever they were close and he continually forced himself against her while they danced. Finally at the door of her hotel room, which she was thankful that she was sharing with another girl, she had to kick him hard to prevent him from forcing his way in. But in spite of his deplorable behavior she felt an attraction towards him. He brought her flowers on her last day in Orlando with a note asking for her forgiveness. He hung his head in shame while apologizing for his display of disrespect, and promised her that he would never act in a similar manner again if she would just give him one more chance.

She was completely sucked in.

Emily returned home to Spanish Wells in a daze. She was sure that she was in love. That Jack was the man she would marry. Their romance became her fixation as she imagined their life together in Florida. Jack had told her that he was attending medical school with the intention of graduating as a doctor specializing in children's care.

What a wonderful devoted man he was!

They sent e-mails on a daily basis, sometimes several a day, they discussed their future together, the number of kids they wanted and Emily even supplied a list of the names that she had chosen for their offspring. Jack agreed to all her suggestions.

What a wonderful considerate man he was!

Derek Hawkins

She imagined her life as a successful doctor's wife living in a pristine community in Florida and earning the respect of her neighbors for the dedication to his work that her husband demonstrated. She envisioned her role in the neighborhood as a pretty young homemaker married to a man who would be the envy of all the other women. She counted her blessings and thanked God for bringing her and Jack together.

What a truly blessed man he was!

Jack wasn't a bad person. He wasn't a thief or a crook. He was quite normal, in his way of thinking. He had a gift with the opposite sex and he used this gift for his own gain. Not monetary gain but for the pure satisfaction of animal conquest. Emily intrigued him. She was young, innocent, naïve and he was sure a virgin. He had to have her. It was that simple with him and he would do just about anything to complete his mission. If only he could have dedicated himself to a worthwhile endeavor with such determination and drive he could have easily become a successful man in whatever field he chose. As you may have already guessed, Jack was not at medical school or any other type of school, he had dropped out of high school when he was fourteen and earned a living doing odd jobs related to the construction industry or parking cars at the Marriott Hotel. He lived at home with his divorced mother in a seedy part of town, where he was surrounded by a conglomerate of others just like him, all of whom looked up to Jack for his exploits with the opposite sex. His escapades and lurid stories were always the best and they looked forward to hearing Jack regale the details of his most recent conquest. He was a hero among the town's losers.

In spite of his arrogance, his single-mindedness and his obsession with all things relating to girls, Jack did have a few commendable qualities. He was a hard worker, a quick learner and an opportunist. He could juggle a hundred metaphorical balls in the air of his brain and keep then all in balance, never at a loss to retrieve the correct response to any question that related to any of the many girls he liked to think that he kept in his stable. In this one field he showed an extraordinary expertise, continually confounding his mates and hoodwinking his sexual partners.

He regularly worked the early morning shift at the Marriott parking garage where his good looks and smiling face were welcomed by most of the regular patrons, especially the women. His favorite car was the white Mercedes convertible that he parked every morning for the elegant lady who ran the boutique in the lobby of the hotel. He was smart enough to recognize the small emblem that was fastened inconspicuously to the inside of the windshield. The emblem was the blue, black and gold of the Bahamian flag. Jack decided to question her about the flag the next time that he saw her. The opportunity arose the following morning.

"I hope you don't think that I'm being too forward," Jack said humbly, "but why do you have a Bahamian flag pasted to your windshield?"

"My husband and I have a home there," she replied with a warm smile.

"That must be nice," commented Jack. "My girlfriend is Bahamian."

"She is?" exclaimed the lady. "Is she from Nassau?"

"No, she's from a little island named Spanish Wells. I doubt that you've ever heard of it."

"Ah, you're wrong. I know it well. Our home is in Harbour Island, right around the corner," she grinned. "How often do you get to see her?"

"Not often enough," replied Jack sadly. "It's too expensive to fly back and forth."

Jack's forlorn expression had the exact effect on her that he knew that it would have. He had touched her heart.

"Our yacht takes us right through Spanish Wells on our way to Harbour Island. I'll ask my husband to take you along with us," she offered.

"Wow, thanks," Jack beamed. "When are you going again?"

"Next month," she answered. "I'll let you know."

As soon as Jack finished his shift he rushed home to send the following message to Emily.

'A buddy of mine has agreed to drop me off for a weekend in Spanish Wells. Look for a big yacht, I'll be on it!'

Emily read the brief message over and over. Jack was coming to see her! His pending visit obliged her to confide in her mother about Jack.

"I met him in Orlando," she told her mother hesitantly. "He's really nice."

"How old is he?" her mother asked unemotionally.

"Eighteen," Emily responded quietly, knowing that eighteen qualified Jack as a man not a boy in her mother's eyes.

Actually Jack was twenty two. He had only told Emily that he was eighteen after he had discovered that she was just fifteen.

"Is he at school?" asked Emily's mother.

"Medical school," stated Emily proudly, "He's studying to be a doctor."

"That's nice. We'll need to meet him when he's here. Invite him to dinner on Saturday."

"Oh thanks Mummy," cried Emily gratefully "I know you'll love him."

Emily sent a message to Jack.

'I told my Mummy all about you, well not all; she wants to meet you and has invited you to dinner on Saturday. Put on a clean shirt and your most winning smile.'

Jack wrote back,

'Just one condition. If I agree to come to dinner you must agree to sleep with me.'

Emily replied,

'I can hardly wait. But you must wear a condom!'

Jack was excited in spite of himself. She's nothing special he told himself, just a pretty kid who wants to get laid. But he couldn't get her out of his mind and when he finally encountered the Mercedes lady he found himself eager to learn of her itinerary. She told him that they would be departing a week from Saturday from Bahia Mar in Fort Lauderdale and that he was expected at six in the morning.

"If the whether is good we'll be there by three in the afternoon," she advised him.

On the appointed day Jack left in the wee hours of the morning in order to arrive at the marina by six. All the stores were closed and he neglected to buy any condoms. 'I'll buy them when I get there' he decided. He felt a little out of place as he was welcomed aboard the yacht. It had to be at least a hundred feet long with a little helicopter on the top deck. Jack was scared to touch anything for fear that he might break something or worse still, make a mark on the polished floors. He removed his shoes and tip-toed around as the mate gave him a tour.

"You can sit here," he was told as a seat on the upper deck was indicated. "Call me if you need anything, Sir."

Jack finally closed his mouth, it had been agape in amazement ever since he had boarded, and took his assigned place.

"This is the life," he called to anyone who happened to be close. No one answered his call except for a pair of seagulls who hovered close by looking for breakfast.

He heard the yacht's engines rumble into life. He watched as she was maneuvered out of her berth into the Intracoastal Waterway. They passed under the Seventeenth Street Bridge, where they were dwarfed by several large cruise ships, and then out to the open sea. The ocean was dead calm and soon the vessel was cruising along at her optimum speed.

"Is everything OK?"

Jack turned in his seat to find the Mercedes lady behind him. She was removing her wrap to reveal a miniscule bikini that barely covered her surprisingly beautiful body.

"I think that I've died and gone to heaven," grinned Jack. He watched in admiration as she settled herself into a position out of the wind where she could obtain the full benefit of the sun's rays.

"Be a dear and rub this lotion on my back please," she asked.

"Sure," stammered Jack as her took the sun block cream from her hand and proceeded to apply it liberally to her silky skin. She purred with contentment.

"How old are you Jack?" she inquired.

"Twenty-eight," he lied.

"Perfect" she mumbled. Jack wasn't sure if she was referring to his age or the movement of his hands. She stretched like a cat on the chaise, unfastening her bikini top as she turned to face him.

"You like?" she teased.

Jack was speechless for the first time in his life.

"You must call me when you get back. I want to hear all about your little girl friend," she mocked and ended their conversation.

After entering the channel into Spanish Wells, the yacht slowed to a crawl before tying up to the Supermarket dock to allow Jack to disembark. Emily was there to greet him. The Mercedes lady waved from her position on the upper deck and blew him a kiss.

"Who's she?" asked Emily suspiciously.

"The owner's wife," answered Jack. She's a nice lady."

"She looks it," commented Emily coolly.

"Forget about her, it's you I came to see."

Emily drove to the Adventures Hotel where she had reserved a room for Jack. The room held some significance for her as it was to be the scene of their lovemaking and the place where she would lose her virginity later that evening.

"Nice room," commented Jack as he felt the softness of the bed. He reached out for Emily and pulled her to him, kissing her neck and rubbing himself against her thighs.

Emily pulled herself away saying, "Later Jack, after dinner with my folks. I've got to go now but I'll be back to pick you up at six. Please behave yourself and look your best."

After she had gone Jack checked with the girl at the front desk as to the location of a drug store. She informed him that the pharmacy was just a short walk from the end of the road.

Jack waited at the counter for the small crowd to leave and for the pharmacist to replace the female assistant at the counter. He was more comfortable speaking to a fellow man.

"Can I help you?" the pharmacist inquired.

"D'you sell condoms?' Jack asked boldly.

"Of course. Singles, a pack of three or a box of twelve" the man replied. "Are you visiting?"

"I just arrived on that big yacht. I'm here to satisfy a cute young local girl who's just begging to get laid by an expert like me," Jack bragged. "I better have a dozen because I know that once she gets a taste of me she won't be able to control herself, she'll want me over and over again."

The Kantaberry Tales

Jack made his purchase and swaggered out of the store to the disgust of the pharmacist who was shaking his head in disbelief.

The tantalizing smells emanating from the kitchen made Jack realize how hungry he was. Emily's mother had greeted him at the door and was constantly stealing glances at him at every opportunity that arose as if she was trying to figure out what it was that her daughter found so attractive about this young man. They sat down at the table at six and waited for Emily's Father to appear. The food was ready before them. Emily's Mother checked her watch and sipped her kantaberry wine.

"He'll be here in a minute," she said hopefully.

"He's never this late," explained Emily.

They continued to wait as the food cooled down. After another five minutes Emily's mother suggested that they begin without her husband.

"Something must have happened," she said "Emily will you give the blessing?"

Emily had not uttered a word, when the door burst open and her Father rushed in apologizing for his tardiness. He took his place at the head of the table and proceeded to give the blessing himself. Nobody noticed Jack's discomfort during Emily's Father's late entry as Jack bowed his head deep into his chest. The blessing ended. Jack continued to bow his head in prayer. A minute passed and Jack had not moved. Five minutes ticked by. Jack was still in the same position with his head bowed deep into his chest and his hands covering his eyes.

"Jack," Emily whispered. "You never told me that you were so religious!"

"And you never told me that your Father was a pharmacist!" he answered hoarsely

ABOUT THE AUTHOR

Derek Hawkins was born and raised in London where he attended London University before emigrating to Canada. He has traveled extensively throughout the Bahamas and the world, finally settling down in Spanish Wells to live and operate a fish farm and fish hatchery.